"So you're female after all, Cassie."

Joel's mocking words cut into Cassie like lashes. "Why are you doing this?" she asked him, unable to choke back the pain-filled demand.

"You're my wife, and since my girlfriend is not prepared to share my bed as long as I remain married, it seems only fair that you should take her place."

Cassie no longer wondered about the source of the chained violence she had sensed in Joel the moment he touched her. "This wasn't part of our agreement," she told him numbly. "I don't want this from you."

"Very well, my virgin wife," he taunted curtly. "But perhaps you ought to have a taste of what you're refusing."

Before she could move he had pinned her back against the bed, the full weight of his body hard against hers, enveloping her in a fiercely sexual tide of mingled rage and need.

Books by Penny Jordan

These books may be available at your local bookseller.

Don't miss any of our special offers. Write to us at the following address for information on our newest releases.

Harlequin Reader Service
P.O. Box 52040, Phoenix, AZ 85072-2040
Canadian address: P.O. Box 2800, Postal Station A,
5170 Yonge St., Willowdale, Ont. M2N 6J3

PENNY JORDAN

taken over

Harlequin Books

TORONTO • NEW YORK • LONDON
AMSTERDAM • PARIS • SYDNEY • HAMBURG
STOCKHOLM • ATHENS • TOKYO • MILAN

Harlequin Presents first edition September 1985
ISBN 0-373-10818-4

Original hardcover edition published in 1985
by Mills & Boon Limited

CHAPTER ONE

'CASSIETRONIC Enterprises'. As always Cassie couldn't quite prevent the excited leap of her heart as she glanced at the name of her company, newly engraved on the brass name plate just inside the prestige office block she had moved in to.

Had anyone told her three years ago that this was where her passion for computer games would lead her she would have scoffed at them. Then, nineteen years old, orphaned and very, very lonely she had entered the competition which had started her on her present road to success, in a mood of lonely defiance.

She hadn't won that competition; she had come second, but looking back she was glad to be the loser because all the winner had to show for his skill was a job with Howard Electronics whilst she ... She glanced again at the nameplate, her heart swelling with pride. If it hadn't been for that chance meeting with David Bennett as she was collecting her prize ... but why dwell on might-have-beens today of all days. She had met David, and he with his accountancy and financial skill had encouraged her to start her own business. This was her third year in business and she had more than rewarded David's faith in her. Only last week a prestigious financial paper had run an article on Cassietronics, praising her flair for designing innovative new games and adaptations. Unwittingly Cassie frowned. All the publicity she had been receiving lately had had its adverse side too. She glanced down at her left hand and smiled as she caught the cold flash of her diamond engagement ring. One more month and Cassietronic would be safely installed under the umbrella of Peter's father's larger company, and safe from any further takeover approaches by Howard Electronics.

As she thought about Howard Electronics she frowned again, remembering how exasperated David had been by her point blank refusal to even discuss their terms. 'But Cassie, they're the best in the field,' he had argued, 'way, way ahead of Pentaton.'

In her heart of hearts Cassie knew that he was right. Joel Howard the brains behind Howard Electronics had a world wide reputation as a computer genius, whereas Peter, skilled though he was, was merely a good technician. Cassie knew that David couldn't understand her preference for Pentatons; 'a second class company, fast losing ground' was how he had scathingly described them, but as Peter had enthusiastically pointed out, with her skill they could soon rebuild and expand their reputation; as his wife and the originator of Cassietronics she would be given a free hand with the future of her own company, and she would also be protected from any more takeover bids such as the one she had just been forced to endure from Joel Howard.

She knew that David would find it difficult to understand her antipathy towards Joel Howard. In David's eyes Howard Electronics was everything Cassie could wish for—a safe harbour for her small company; a chance to expand and extend her range with the security of Howard Electronics' financial backing behind her.

But nothing comes from nothing, Cassie had learned that lesson young, from an embittered father who had spent the best years of his life, standing helplessly by while an incompetent brother-in-law ran down, and eventually destroyed the company his father had handed down to him as his son, rather than into the hands of his far more competent but not related by blood, son-in-law. Cassie had never known if her father had married her mother purely because he wanted the company—she hoped not—but what she did know was that by the time she was ten years old her father, the brilliant maths lecturer, who had married one of his students and given up a promising career in order to help run his father-in-law's company, had been reduced to the status of a cipher within that company, his pride destroyed; embittered by the wasteland that his life had become.

The year Cassie was ten the company had gone bankrupt; her mother had had a nervous breakdown and her father had had to return to teaching, but not this time as a respected university lecturer with all the privileges and power that entailed. The only post he had been able to obtain had been at the same huge comprehensive school Cassie attended and she had watched the disillusionment of what he had become slowly destroy her father.

Her mother had died when she was thirteen, slowly fading away until one day she simply released her hold on life, and with her father as her sole parent Cassie had learned from him the bitter lessons of his life. In his daughter he had discovered the same aptitude for maths that he had, and this skill had been honed and polished until Cassie far outstripped her fellow pupils. This had carried its own penance. It wasn't 'done' for a girl to be even moderately good at maths, never mind brilliant enough to outstrip even the more senior pupils, and torn between pleasing her father and gaining the acceptance of her peers Cassie had gradually taught herself to accept that there would always be a gulf between herself and her schoolmates. Most of them treated her as though she were an alien life-form, teasing and tormenting her until she gradually withdrew from them to the extent where their barbs never touched her.

While her fellow students flirted and dated Cassie concentrated on her maths, and it had been from this that her interest in the new technology had sprung. Her father died the year she was nineteen from a heart attack, and it had been in a mood of bitter defiance at life following his death that she had entered the competition.

Her ability to design and pioneer computer games was something that still half amazed her. She had discovered in herself a deep hidden vein of imagination which, when harnessed to her mathematical skills, made her games far superior to those of her rivals.

'Don't ever forget that while you're at the top of the tree now,' David had warned her seriously, 'computer games is a young people's industry. One day you will grow stale, and you must prepare yourself for that day.'

She had already earned enough money not to need to worry about her financial future, and as Peter's wife ... She frowned, sighing faintly as she stepped into the lift which would take her up to her suite of offices. Her last game had been almost frighteningly successful. It had sent her company's profits soaring, and it had been then that she first realised the dangerous waters her success was taking her into.

Other established companies had started casting envious eyes in her direction, especially the two leaders in the field, Howard Electronics and Peter's father's company Pentaton. She still seethed inwardly thinking of her one and only meeting—if it could be called that—with Joel Howard.

He had strolled into her office, smiling winningly at her as she lifted her head to look at him. Tall, at least six foot two, with an almost overwhelming breadth of shoulder, something inside her had retreated from him on sight. Brief memories of the agonies of her schooldays; the scorn of her class-mates and the taunting mockery of boys who had no doubt grown up into men like Joel Howard; arrogant; assured, all too aware of their sexual magnetism, surfaced and flooded out into reality, and as his navy-blue eyes skimmed over her she had been burningly aware of the plainness of her features; of her untidy cascade of mid-brown hair; the lack of elegance of her too thin five-foot-six frame; the dullness of her pale skin without make-up and the depressing ordinaryness of her hazel eyes behind the screen of the huge glasses which, in her moments of vanity, she deluded herself she needed only for close work.

That one considering look had summed her up and dismissed her—humiliatingly, the mocking warmth of his smile merely adding to the pain of the memories the sight of him stirred up. Once, long long ago she had fallen deeply in love—an adolescent crush, she recognised now, and only she could have been stupid enough to fall for the most sought-after boy in school; a boy who had made capital out of her badly hidden feelings for him, turning her into a laughing stock for his cronies. Her skin burned at the memory, and while being aware of it she had glared at Joel Howard with all the pent-up hatred of those times in her eyes.

'My, my dragon lady,' he had drawled, almost insultingly, she remembered, 'whatever have I done to you? Or is it just the male race in general that you hate? I'd like to see your boss,' he had told her, not bothering to smile this time, but eyeing her instead with cool, sardonically knowing eyes. 'She is expecting me. My secretary made an appointment.'

Already he was looking beyond Cassie to the closed door of the inner office that was really hers. She had come into the outer office to use her secretary's typewriter, and the bitter knowledge of how Joel Howard would view the reality of her identity had suddenly struck her. While he thought she was merely a secretary he had made no secret of his sexual contempt for her. When he discovered who she really was, no doubt he would use all the flattery and sexual skill he undoubtedly possessed to persuade her to give him what he wanted—and that wasn't her. A mirthless laugh shook her slender body, racking it with pain. Oh no, men like Joel Howard didn't want plain drabs of women like her. Joel Howard went for the glamorous model and actress type, she had seen his photograph in various periodicals, escorting them. He was known as the playboy king of the computer world. A man who had made a fortune by the time he was twenty-five, and who had gone on using his skill to expand his business empire until he was one of the two largest in the country. The other largest company was the one owned by Peter's family— an older, less go-ahead company according to David, but she would rather sell her soul to the devil than ally herself to Joel Howard in any way, Cassie thought bitterly.

She didn't want to remember the shrewdly assessing way in which his glance had slid over her tense body when she delivered the bombshell of her identity, but as she stepped out of the lift and into her office she couldn't prevent herself doing so. He had stood there, towering over her, making her wish she had the forethought to stand up before she had told him. His suit was dark, and made of the finest, softest wool, fitting impeccably, as did his silk shirt. On the outside, he was the epitome of the successful businessman, but Cassie wasn't deceived; at heart he was a hunter, a powerful, cruel predator, who would stop at nothing to get what he wanted, and he wanted her company. Cassie had sensed that straight away, and a renewing surge of power had given her the courage to stand up to him, to deny the potent force of the charm he was directing at her, using to cloak a willpower so formidable that she could practically feel it reaching out to subdue her.

Afterwards when she had questioned David he had admitted that for once Joel Howard had bitten off slightly more than he could chew; that his investments in advanced, as yet undeveloped futuristic technology had drained his companies of capital reserves, and that if he wasn't to be forced into abandoning his research he would have to come up with a market leader, and very quickly.

'It isn't Joel's fault,' David had assured her. 'One of his top designers broke his contract and accepted a job in Silicone Valley—California,' he had elucidated. 'He took with him the new computer game he had been working on as part of Joel's design team. Open industrial piracy, but there wasn't a thing Joel could do about it.'

'So now he's decided to indulge in a little piracy of his own,' Cassie had interrupted bitterly, 'he wants my company——'

'He wants to take you over, yes,' David had agreed, mildly puzzled by the vehemency of her voice. 'But I warned you you would have to expect this Cassie. You're in an extremely vulnerable position at the moment—a very tempting and tasty little minnow surrounded by a dozen or more greedy dangerous sharks . . .'

'And the law of the jungle being what it is, the biggest and greediest gets to gobble me up—well not this time,' Cassie had told him emphatically.

David had tried hard to change her mind. 'He's the best in his field, Cassie,' he had pointed out. 'I can't see what you've got against him.'

'I can't see us working together,' Cassie had

told him firmly. 'He strikes me as the type of man who believes the best place for a woman is in the kitchen . . .'

She had said it scathingly, hurt and offended when David had smothered a totally male smile. Her mind made up in that instant that no matter how much David cajoled she would not allow Howard Electronics to swallow up her company.

It had been ten days after that that she had been approached by Peter Williams. She had liked him on sight, warmed by his sympathetic, hesitant manner, readily agreeing to a dinner date with him, flattered and encouraged by the interest and admiration he showed in her.

A month later he had asked her to marry him and she had agreed. Cassie had no illusions about herself. Peter would never have wanted to marry her if it hadn't been for her company, but if she was honest with herself would she have agreed to marry him if it hadn't been for her pressing need to protect it from Joel Howard's aggressive greed?

It didn't strike her as odd that she should be marrying simply for reasons of convenience. She liked Peter and they would work well together. Hopefully they would have children, although her mind withdrew timidly from the thought of physical intimacies between them. Peter had only kissed her on half a dozen or so occasions, his mouth dry and tentative, arousing only the mildest sensation of curiosity inside her.

So she had a very low sex drive; she shrugged off the waiting pain; hadn't she always known that? And wasn't it fortunate in the circumstances? There could be nothing worse than a

plain woman longing to be made passionate love
to, wasting all her life waiting for her knight on a
white charger. No, although it hurt to be realistic,
in the long run it was safer. She already had far
more than she had ever expected. She had her
independence; both financial and physical, and as
she had learned from her father, that was the
most important and most enduring thing in life.
He had surrendered his to his wife's family and
had never ceased to regret it.

She and Peter had discussed their future
carefully. She would continue to run
Cassietronics independently of his father's company. Peter would continue to work for his
father. They would buy a flat in London, close to
her office and then perhaps later she would work
from home.

She had everything she had always wanted,
Cassie told herself as she riffled through her mail,
ignoring the small, nagging pain that suddenly
surfaced in the memory of that tall dark-haired
boy from school. How her heart and body had
ached every time she looked at him. She had
dreamed of his kiss, of his touch; mildly erotic
painful dreams that robbed her of concentration.
It was as well she had had that lesson, she told
herself firmly as she applied herself to her post.
She was a very wealthy young woman now, and a
very vulnerable one. If she hadn't had her dreams
and illusions smashed then she could easily have
been in danger of falling for some smooth-
tongued opportunist who wanted her merely for
her wealth.

Her aunt had warned her often enough recently
that that was what could happen to her. Cassie

sighed and pushed her letters to one side as she thought about Aunt Renee, her uncle's widow. Bitterly resentful of the company's failure, she blamed Cassie's father for its downfall, conveniently overlooking the fact that her husband had been the one responsible for its demise. Uncle Ted was dead now like her father, and Aunt Renee, although only an aunt by marriage, was the only relative she had left. Sometimes Cassie felt as though her aunt hated her. She was bitterly vindictive about Cassie's father, and never lost an opportunity of reminding Cassie how plain she was. Once beautiful herself she still had remnants of that beauty. She spent a fortune on clothes and at beauty salons, using the money Uncle Ted had left her to finance exotic holidays. Invariably when Cassie saw her she was being escorted by a much younger, far too handsome man. As a teenager Cassie had suffered cruelly from her malicious jibes.

Telling herself that she had missed nothing by not being beautiful Cassie suddenly froze as she flipped over a magazine and Joel Howard's handsome face smiled back at her. Beneath the photograph was an article about a charity 'do' he had been attending and included in the picture was a petite, pretty blonde. Cassie's mouth curled disdainfully. Why was it when men like Joel Howard used their wealth and position to buy themselves pretty little playthings that the rest of the male world looked on in approving envy, yet when a woman did exactly the same thing, she was scorned and derided for it?

There was no such thing as equality for the sexes, Cassie thought bitterly ignoring the stab-

bing of her conscience which told her that Joel
Howard would attract beautiful women even if he
didn't have a penny to his name. There was about
him an aura of sexual magnetism that even *she*
could sense, and wasn't he just aware of it? That
was why she disliked him so much, Cassie
thought disdainfully. She loathed and despised
the way he made capital out of his too obvious
good looks. Yes, that's right, she despised him,
she told herself, savouring the thought, starting
suddenly when the telephone rang abruptly.

She picked up the receiver, relaxing when she
heard Peter's gentle voice. What had she
expected, she mocked herself. To hear Joel
Howard's deeply masculine, taunting voice? He
wouldn't approach her again. Not after the
emphatic refusal to even talk to him she had
given to David.

Peter was ringing to confirm the arrangements
for their date that night. They were going out to
celebrate their as yet unpublicised engagement,
and to make arrangements for their wedding at
the end of the month. Not until she was actually
married to Peter would she feel completely safe,
Cassie thought as she replaced the receiver. Safe?
She frowned a little, force of habit encouraging
her to analyse her emotions. From what or whom
should she need to feel safe? Against her will her
eyes were drawn to Joel Howard's photograph
and she stared blindly at it for several minutes
before finally tearing her gaze away.

She was late leaving the office, primarily because
of an idea she had suddenly had that she couldn't
wait to start working on. It was only when she

happened to glance at her watch and realised the time that she had reluctantly left her computer.

Now she had barely half an hour in which to get ready for their date. Guilt smote her as she remembered the hair appointment she had made. She had wanted to look her best for Peter tonight, feeling that she owed it to him to make some special effort on his behalf. She knew why he was marrying her. It couldn't be easy for him. She sighed faintly, studying her face in her mirror. Every feature was unremarkable save perhaps for the size and shape of her eyes and the delicate bone structure of her body, but Cassie could see no virtue in these. She was too thin; too pale and just generally too uninteresting.

When she had showered and put on clean underwear she opened her wardrobe doors. All the clothes inside it had been chosen for their anonymity; chosen to help her blend into a crowd and thus escape any criticism. Selecting a mushroom beige dress she tugged it on and fastened it. The loose, shapeless style disguised her slimness covering her from wrists to knees in dull beige. Against the dress her skin looked paler than ever, her hair even more mousy. Cassie normally wore it up in a neat chignon and she gathered it into this style with the ease of long practice. At one time she had worn it in one long plait, but she had been so teased for this at university that she had adopted a more mature style. She had once toyed with the idea of wearing contact lenses, but as she told herself that really she needed her glasses only for close work she had abandoned this idea. She put them on to apply a brief covering of make-up, adding her lipstick almost mechanically, wondering why it was that make-up did so little for her. A brief spray of the rich, oriental perfume Peter had bought for her, and she was ready. That the perfume did not suit her at all, did not concern her, Peter had chosen it and therefore she felt she must wear it.

She glanced down at the large solitaire weighing down her slender finger and picked up her coat. She was just putting it on when she heard her door.

Peter smiled when he saw her, leaning forward to give her a dutiful peck on her cheek. She couldn't imagine Joel Howard embracing his dates so tamely. The thought made her face flame with anger. Why on earth was she thinking about him?

'Ready?'

She nodded and smiled, following Peter outside.

'My parents went on ahead to the restaurant,' he told her with a smile. 'My car's outside.'

Peter's parents. Cassie's heart sank. She wasn't too keen on her in-laws-to-be, finding Peter's father brash and overbearing, and his mother another potential Aunt Renee. She knew that Isabel Williams was disappointed in her only son's choice of wife; and she also sensed that even though Ralph Williams was pleased by the match, he was contemptuous of her as a woman. Sometimes Cassie felt that she wanted to scream that it wasn't her fault that she was plain; that she still had feelings and could still be hurt, but she squashed the impulse. As she followed Peter into his car she found herself stifling the reckless

desire to turn to him and demand that he kissed
her, really kissed her. What on earth was the
matter with her? She shivered despite the warmth
of the car and Peter was instantly concerned.

'It's time I got a new car,' he told her,
frowning. 'This one's had it, but father replaced
his Rolls earlier this year. Perhaps you could buy
me a new car as a wedding present?'

Cassie knew that he was only teasing but
somehow the words grated. She was getting over-
sensitive, she told herself. She had entered this
engagement willingly enough; she had known
why Peter had proposed; she couldn't claim that
she loved him any more than he loved her, so
why this feeling of distaste; this desire to open
the car door and run?

Bridal nerves? She smiled derisively. Hadn't
her father brought her up to face the truth about
herself, no matter how painful? She was a plain,
clever woman, whose fiancé was marrying her
because of her cleverness rather than her beauty.
Was that really any worse than being married for
beauty? Beauty faded, ability lasted . . . so who
really was the loser; the beauty or the blue-
stocking?

Sighing, Cassie realised that they had reached
the restaurant. Peter looked very attractive in his
dinner suit, his fair hair gleaming under the lights
in the foyer. It wasn't his fault that despite his
boyish good looks there was a weak, almost
petulant droop to his mouth. He had been spoiled
by his mother, Cassie knew; and she also
suspected that Isabel Williams fully intended to
carry on that spoiling after their marriage.

The restaurant was a popular one and full.

They were shown to their table where Peter's parents were waiting for them. Isabel Williams made a big show of kissing Cassie enthusiastically, but Cassie could see the rejection in her eyes, the smug female satisfaction in the younger woman's plainness, and as she studied her mother-in-law-to-be's immaculate make-up and expensive silk dress Cassie was acutely conscious of her own plain appearance.

Once their meal was ordered Isabel started to discuss plans for the wedding.

'Talk to Cassie about that some other time,' Ralph Williams ordered his wife. 'Cassie, I want to set up a meeting between our two accountants . . .' He went on talking and Cassie was suddenly and acutely conscious of being studied by someone outside their table.

So intense was the sensation of being watched that her skin prickled underneath it. She itched to turn round but refused to give in to the impulse, forcing herself to listen to Peter's father. He was asking her about the work she had in progress, enquiring if she was working on anything new. She was just about to demur, hating talking about what she was doing until it was clear in her own mind, when she felt an overwhelming urge to turn round seize her. She had given in to it almost before she was aware of doing so, her breath catching in her throat as her glance clashed with the navy-blue stare of Joel Howard. He was seated two tables away, just simply watching her, oblivious to the chatter of his blonde companion. The look in his eyes was so savagely angry that Cassie rocked with the force of it. It was like shouting defiance at thunder and lightning, and her mind reeled away from the shattering impact of his anger. She had known he was angry at her refusal to talk to him, but the intensity of that rage was something she had not anticipated. It was several seconds before she could draw her glance away and in that time Peter became conscious of her lack of attention.

'Joel Howard,' he exclaimed in disgust, 'what on earth is he doing here?'

His father spun round, frowning angrily at the other table. 'He wants Cassietronics.' He said it loudly enough for the other man to hear, and Cassie caught the flash of fury darken the navy-blue eyes to black. Fear, and something else coursed through her body, making her shake and cling to the safe security of Peter's fingers. The stone in her engagement ring glittered and she could almost feel the instant Joel Howard's attention became fixed on it, the expression on his face changing, hardening first to rage and then to contemptuous derision.

Quite distinctly above the murmur of conversation from the other tables Cassie heard his companion complaining, 'Darling, what's wrong? You look dreadfully angry.'

She could just hear Joel's response, and as the cruelty of it drove what colour there was from her face, she knew that it had been pitched deliberately for her to hear it.

'Nothing's wrong,' he told the blonde, 'I was just thinking that some men would sell their very souls, not to mention their lives, to get what they want.'

The blonde pouted, and Cassie couldn't drag her eyes away even though she desperately wanted to. 'Would you?' she asked him archly. Across the intervening tables, his eyes locked on Cassie's, contempt and derision mingling.

'Not in this particular case,' he drawled, and Cassie knew the words were meant for her. 'There are some prices too high for any man to pay.' His gaze left her face to slide contemptuously over her body and where she had been pale Cassie was now hot, with humiliation and rage; so bitter and angry that she was shaking with it. At her side Ralph Williams said something, and remembering his earlier question she replied brightly and a little too loudly.

'As a matter of fact I am working on something new—it's going to be a wedding present for Peter.' She flashed a bright and totally meaningless smile at her fiancé, barely aware of what she was saying as she told him, 'If it's anywhere near as successful as my last one darling, it will buy you a whole fleet of new cars—and the garages to go with them.'

Ordinarily Cassie would have been appalled by her behaviour, shrinking away from the crassness of it, but right now, all she cared about was wiping the derisive glitter from Joel Howard's eyes; she wanted to see him humiliated as he had just humiliated her. Without saying the words he had told her plainly that in his eyes she had bought herself a husband; and that no woman would ever be allowed to buy him.

The rest of the meal passed in a daze. She drank champagne, she knew that, and she listened to toasts on their engagement. Later she and Peter danced, but although he held her close to his body, murmuring his delight at her earlier

words, excitement making his body tense against
hers, in reality she was far away from him,
concentrating on the sight of Joel Howard,
dancing with his blonde companion. Her head
barely reached his shoulder and their bodies
swayed together as intimately as though they had
been making love ... As they would make love
later on. Cassie's head swam with the intensity of
her thoughts: she shivered in Peter's arms,
shaking with revulsion at the direction of her
thoughts. They were an invasion of the other
couple's privacy; almost voyeuristic in their
intensity and they shamed her to her soul. What
was it about Joel Howard that prompted such a
reaction from her; that drove her beyond the
boundaries of logic and reason into a realm where
emotions alone held sway?

She was relieved when the time came for them
finally to leave. She was just waiting for Peter in
the foyer when she felt iron fingers curl round
her arm. She froze instantly, knowing with a
knowledge that went beyond logic whose fingers
they were.

'Why are you marrying him?'

The contempt in his voice lashed her into swift
retaliation. 'I thought you already knew. I'm
buying myself a husband. Peter is a very
attractive man.'

'Attractive enough to make you willing to part
with Cassietronics?' His voice derided her, telling
her that he knew exactly why Peter was marrying
her. She wanted to lash out and hurt him as he
had just hurt her by laying bare the fact that
without her skill, without her company Peter
would never even have looked at her. It was one

thing for *her* to know that, it was another for
someone else; for *him*, to point that out to her,
and suddenly she latched on to the thing that
would wound him the deepest.

Baring her teeth in a parody of a smile, she said
softly, 'Oh no, but knowing that by marrying him
I'm preventing *you* from getting Cassietronics
makes it more than worthwhile.'

She pulled herself free of his grip before he
could retaliate, walking on shaky legs to where
Peter had just emerged from the cloakroom with
her jacket. It was only when they reached the
door that she turned round, impelled by
something stronger than her will to look at Joel
Howard. What she saw in his face made her pale
and sway, shocked by the force of the implacable
determination she saw written there; forced to
acknowledge the message he was sending her
with those cold, hard eyes. She might have
thought she had won, but he hadn't given up the
fight yet. He still wanted her company; and he
still meant to have it, with or without her consent.

As she settled into Peter's car she was attacked
by a cowardly desire to beg him to marry her
tomorrow; but she fought against the impulse
telling herself that she was reacting foolishly
emotionally. What could Joel Howard really do?
Nothing, nothing at all.

CHAPTER TWO

IT was almost a week since Peter had taken her out to dinner with his parents; almost a week since she had seen Joel Howard, and in that short space of time he had occupied far too many of her thoughts Cassie reflected, angered by her own inability to dismiss the man from her mind.

This afternoon she had an appointment for the first fitting of her wedding dress. Peter's mother had made all the arrangements and Cassie glared resentfully at the entry in her diary, wishing instead that she could spend the afternoon working on her new idea.

It was always like this when a new idea came to her; she wanted to spend all the time she could developing it and it occupied her thoughts to the exclusion of everything else. Not quite everything on this occasion a small voice reminded her; there was the irritating monotony with which Joel Howard interrupted her thought processes.

Damn the man, she thought angrily. Another three weeks and she would be safely married to Peter and Cassietronics would be out of his reach for ever. That must be why she spent so much time thinking about him. That threat of his, unspoken maybe, but very real threat, none the less, was preying on her mind. Her intercom buzzed and she flicked the switch automatically. The voice of her temporary secretary, cool and disembodied reminded her of her afternoon appointment. Her own secretary had been absent with some mysterious ailment for several days but before going off ill she had arranged for a temporary girl to take her place. The temp was almost frighteningly efficient Cassie acknowledged, shrugging on the jacket of her neat tweed suit. She had owned the suit for several years, and although it was unremarkable both in cut and colour, she felt comfortable in it. It helped her to fade into the background. As she moved Peter's ring glittered under the office lighting and she almost flinched from its gleam. It wasn't really her sort of ring at all, far too cold and brash; chosen for show—rather like her marriage an inner voice taunted—but Cassie firmly dismissed it. As yet she and Peter had made no formal announcement to the press of their engagement. Peter's father had suggested they wait until just before the wedding; had in fact told them that he would call a press conference for that day, at which the announcement would be made. Although she had said nothing at the time, Cassie frowned a little, wondering if she was quite happy about the way Peter's father seemed to be ruling their lives. Peter was weak where his parents were concerned, and although initially that had not worried her, gradually she was coming to see their power over him as a cause for concern. What would happen if there were ever to be a clash between Pentaton's interests and those of Cassietronics? Would Peter support her?

Telling herself that she was just suffering from pre-nuptuil nerves Cassie let herself out of her office. The temporary secretary; a tall, attractive brunette smiled at her, but Cassie ignored her smile. The other girl was poised and attractive, her very self-confidence making Cassie miserably aware of her own short-comings. Although she was only wearing a very simple skirt and blouse the rich emerald colour provided a stark contrast for Cassie's own drab oatmeal outfit.

Would there ever come a day when the sight of a pretty woman didn't immediately underline and reinforce her own insecurities Cassie wondered bitterly, as she left the office.

Her car was parked in the basement car park, and she had already told the temp that she didn't expect to be back that afternoon. In the capacious bag she always carried with her were the notes she had jotted down for her new game. Perhaps this evening she would get an opportunity to work on them. The initial stages of creating a new game were always very absorbing, and as she pressed the basement button in the lift Cassie felt her doubts and dreads slip away as she was filled with the familiar tide of exultation a new venture always brought her.

By the time she stepped out of the lift she was feeling much more optimistic. The basement was murkily dark after the bright light of the lift, and while she waited for her eyes to adjust she made her way automatically to her parking bay. As she reached her car she frowned over the selfish way in which the owner of the next bay had parked his vehicle, almost, but not quite blocking her in. The car was unfamiliar to her, long and sleek, its black paintwork glittering almost menacingly.

As she drew nearer she recognised its distinctive trademark and her mouth curled disdainfully. A Ferrari, no doubt the proud possession of some image-conscious, successful businessman occupying one of the other offices. Without bothering to give it another glance Cassie extracted her keys from her bag and bent to insert them into the lock.

The totally unexpected pressure of strong fingers on her arm made her freeze, her heart thudding in instinctive terror as fear drove a surge of adrenalin through her veins. Without stopping to think or reason Cassie tried to pull away, fear clawing frantically inside her. Her free hand lashed out at her foe, palm and fingers smarting from the blow she managed to land against a frighteningly hard torso.

'Stop it, I don't intend to hurt you.' Her free hand was tethered, imprisoned with its fellow behind her back in the same instant that she was spun round to face her assailant.

The sight of him was almost as terrifying as discovering his presence. The colour drained from Cassie's face as she stared up into familiar ink-blue eyes and then unwillingly down over a hard boned male face to the grim line of a mouth drawn into a hard curl of disdain.

'If you always react like that when a man touches you, Peter Williams must have been dreading his honeymoon.'

The mocking words infiltrated her brain slowly because it was far too busy trying to come to terms with the identity of her attacker.

'Just as well I'm going to save him the ordeal isn't it?'

Cassie's mind refused to function. She stared disbelievingly up into Joel Howard's face, barely taking in what he was saying.

Still holding her tethered with one hand, he used the other to reach behind him and snap open the passenger door of the Ferrari.

Stupidly Cassie stared at it. 'That's your car?'

Without deigning to answer her he pulled open the door, half pushing and half lifting her into the seat. His actions released Cassie from her frozen state and she started to fight to get free, pushing against the hard muscled wall of his chest as he leaned across her securing the seat belt.

'Stop that.' His voice was curt. 'I don't want to have to use violence, but that doesn't mean I won't, if I need to . . .'

The tone of his voice warned Cassie that he was telling the truth. Abruptly she retreated from him, tensing back in her seat like a small animal trying to curl into a protective ball.

'I don't understand,' she told him shakily. 'What is this all about?'

His car door slammed as he got in beside her, pressing a button. The faint click told Cassie what he had done and she looked wildly at her door reaching for the handle.

'Too late, I've just locked us in.' The laconic voice agitated her already overwrought nerves.

'Will you please tell me what stupid game you think you're playing,' she demanded wildly. 'I'm supposed to be on my way to a fitting for my wedding dress, and you're making me late.'

'Since you won't be wearing it, that hardly matters,' he told her coolly, snapping on his own seat belt and switching on the engine. 'Did you really think I'd sit tamely by and let you destroy everything I'd worked for over the last ten years?'

Muzzily Cassie shook her head, trying to clear

her thoughts. 'I'm not going to let you take over my company, if that's what all this is about,' she told him defiantly. 'And no amount of sweet-talk from you will persuade me. How did you know that I would be here this afternoon?' she demanded, suddenly suspicious.

'Easy. I persuaded your secretary to take a few days off so that mine could monitor your comings and goings.'

'*Your* secretary.' Cassie was bitterly enraged. 'No doubt she much prefers working for you than me,' she told him sarcastically remembering the girl's immaculate grooming and pretty face.

'No doubt,' Joel Howard replied smoothly, 'but she'll be amply rewarded for her efforts.'

His tone and the look that accompanied it gave Cassie the distinct impression that Joel Howard believed that every female alive had her price if one was prepared to pay it. He had, she thought in quick surprise, almost as low an opinion of her sex as she had of his. She frowned, realising the strangeness of this thought. She would have expected a man as sexually compelling as Joel would be a devout admirer of the female sex; after all there was no doubt that he was thoroughly spoiled by it, so why did she have the impression that he despised, even perhaps disliked women.

'And how will you reward her,' she flashed back at him, angered as much by her own thoughts as by his manner. 'In cash or in kind . . .'

She saw his face harden as his hands gripped the wheel of his car.

'Don't try the clever comments on me,' he

advised her harshly. 'It's hardly my fault if your sex is so open to bribery, is it?'

'Throughout the ages women have been forced to use what weapons they can against men, because men persist in considering them their inferiors,' Cassie told him spiritedly, her mouth twisting bitterly as she remembered the price she had been forced to pay for her clever mathematical brain both by her own and the male sex.

'I don't have time to argue semantics right now,' Joel told her hardily, 'we've got an appointment to keep.'

'An appointment?' Cassie's heart leapt in fear. 'You can't force me to sign over my company to you.'

'Susan tells me you're working on a new game.' He had changed the subject completely and there wasn't a thing Cassie could do about it.

She blinked dizzied by their sudden emergence into the daylight, wondering if she could possibly attract someone's attention to the fact that she had been taken prisoner against her will; that she was virtually being abducted by this insufferably arrogant male creature who didn't seem to be able to take 'no' for an answer.

'And if I am?' she responded, refusing to let him see how frightened she really was. Not for herself. She knew he intended her no physical harm. No, it was the compulsive strength of will; the powerful determination cloaked by the sophisticated façade that frightened her. He was, she recognised fearfully, a man who would stop at nothing to get what he wanted. And he wanted her company.

'If it's as successful as your last one, it will turn

Pentatons into the leading electronic games company in the UK.' He took his attention off the road for a second to give her a thin-lipped and bitter look. 'By the same token it will almost completely destroy my company and that's something I cannot allow to happen. I need the revenues and the status of being the number one games company in this country to persuade the government to continue with the aid they've been giving me for several new ventures we're working on. We've almost reached the breakthrough point. Another six months and we'll have cleared the danger point; the first of our new, advanced designs will be through the initial stages and we can make announcements to the press that will secure their future, but all that will only come about if I can maintain my position as market leader for that space of time and if you marry Peter Williams and merge your company, your skill, with Pentaton that will be impossible.' He broke off to turn left, and then smiled at her again, a smile that made her blood run cold. 'So you can see why, I am sure, with that keen, sharp brain of yours why I simply cannot allow you to marry him.'

Petrified though she was Cassie managed to retort coldly, 'And how do you propose to stop me?'

The minute the pert question was asked, she regretted it. She saw from the expression on his face that he was going to enjoy giving her the answer, and a roaring tide of apprehension flooded through her nervous system making her shiver spasmodically.

'Quite simple,' he told her softly, 'I intend to

marry you myself. It's all arranged. I've got the special licence; the ceremony has been organised.'

Cassie's reaction was instinctive and immediate. 'Stop this car at once,' she demanded huskily. 'You must be mad if you think you can get away with this.'

His mirthless laughter chilled her over-heated skin. 'With careful planning and proper fore-thought one can get away with a great deal.'

'You can't make me marry you if I don't want to.' Cassie was appalled to hear her voice tremble, and she knew by the brief, triumphant smile that curved his hard mouth that Joel Howard had spotted her momentary weakness as well.

'I shouldn't be too sure about that if I were you,' he told her, adding almost musingly, 'It's marvellous what they can do with drugs these days, isn't it.'

'You wouldn't drug me?' Cassie was aghast. Surely not even a man like Joel Howard would go to such lengths?

'Not with anything dangerous,' he agreed, stopping the car at traffic lights and turning to watch her. 'But believe me, Cassie, I need this marriage to you. I won't see all my hard work wasted because you're vain and stupid enough to fall for a weakling like Peter Williams. Do you honestly believe he cares about you?'

His question; the scorn in his voice; the intimation that no man worthy of the name could possibly find her attractive, bit into Cassie's pride making her recoil with the pain of the wounds he was causing, but before she could retaliate caution intruded. Joel Howard was dangerous; all the more so for being determined to carry out his plan of action. Cassie wasn't a fool; she could see how much the success of his ventures meant to him and she could also easily believe that he would stop at nothing to achieve that success. Quickly she thought and came up with the only way she could escape her present situation, galling to her pride though it was.

'I'll sell you the company,' she told him with quick bitterness. 'Stop the car and take me back to my office . . .'

'And let you go running to the Williams family for protection?' Joel Howard laughed soundlessly, 'Oh, no, Cassie, there's only one way I can be sure of your loyalty and that's by buying it the same way Peter Williams intended to buy it—by marrying you.'

It was on the tip of Cassie's tongue to deny his assertion that the only way she could get a husband was by exchanging her company for one; and that furthermore the main reason she was marrying Peter was to stop him from taking over Cassietronics, but she quickly saw the pitfalls of such an announcement.

'Peter . . .'

'Loves you?' he derided. 'He loves no one but himself. Have you looked at yourself in the mirror recently, Cassie? Do you really think . . .'

The sheer cruelty of what she was sure he was about to say took Cassie's breath away for a second. Pain, searing and brutally sharp tore through her body, and just for a handful of seconds she longed to make him retract his words; to have him look at her with admiration and awe, to want her as . . . 'No.' Cassie was unaware of her sharply cried denial, her face white and set as she tried to come to terms with her thoughts, shivering in mute reaction to the danger of them. What was she thinking? It was Joel Howard's fault she thought angrily. He had got her in such an emotionally vulnerable state that she didn't know *what* she was thinking. Of course she didn't want him to find her attractive; even if such an improbability were possible she wouldn't want it; she wouldn't want *him*.

'Even if you manage to force me to go through with this farce of a marriage, you won't be able to stop me from going to the Press and telling them the truth,' she told him fiercely, fighting against her emotions and summoning all her reasoning powers to her aid. She would need every ounce of logic and analytical skill she possessed if she was to best this man; an instinct that was purely feminine told her that.

'Go ahead,' he invited drawlingly, 'but you'll be using a two-edged sword if you do. What do you think it will do to your own credibility, to the reputation of your company, if you told the truth and were believed?'

He gave her a few seconds to digest his comment before looking at her again. They were leaving the city behind them now, heading for the Cotswolds Cassie noticed absently as she struggled to find a way to deny his comments.

'All right, so you'd ruin my reputation, but you'd also destroy your own company. There's no one to touch you for computer games in this country and with you out of business my computer games division would be number one again. With confidence restored in our ability to be innovative; to remain leaders of the field, I'd have no problem at all in attracting the finance I need to continue with the other work I have in hand.'

Computer electronics was his field as Cassie knew, and torn between a blazing exhibition of temper and simply saying nothing she burst out bitterly, 'What is this revolutionary something you're working on anyway? Some sort of miracle robot?'

'You're getting warm. I might as well tell you because there's no one else in the field anywhere near advanced to rival us in this development. We've been working on a computer controlled device that can be used for micro surgery. It's faster and better than any human could ever be— both advantages when it comes to sewing back a severed limb or working on delicate areas of the brain, and since it's controlled by the surgeon in charge in effect it's an extension of his hands, accurate and capable of working to the millionth of a degree. Although we do have a lot of support, as with anything new we also have a lot of detractors, people who say that government money would be better spent on more nurses and doctors; hence my concern to ensure that our backers aren't frightened off. With my computer games division demoted to second place those who are against what we're working on will be quick to use it to hold up the flow of funds we need to complete the development.'

For a moment Cassie was awed by what he had told her. Her own skill was something she took for granted; the large revenues it brought her in still sometimes overwhelming, but when all was said and done they were merely games. She felt humbled by what she had just heard and resentful of feeling humbled at the same time.

'Joel . . .' It was the first time she had ever used his name and she caught the faint flutter of surprise crossing his face. 'I've changed my mind,' she told him quickly, 'I will let you take over Cassietronics.'

She was completely sincere in what she had said, believing that what he was working on was far more important than her own dislike of him, but the look on his face turned her humility to anger as he mocked tauntingly, 'That soft, womanly approach has been tried on me by experts, Cassie, and without success. I learned one thing very young and that one thing was never trust a female. For all that you dress like a drab little sparrow you're still a member of the female sex. Oh no, my dear, that won't work. I *do* have the intelligence to realise what you're up to you know. I turn round and drive you back to your office and the moment I leave you it's straight to Peter Williams . . . No . . . There really is no other way.'

'You mean you're prepared to sacrifice your freedom; to marry a plain drab little sparrow purely for altruistic love of your fellow man?' Carrie flung at him bitterly, anger seeping through her as she came up against the brick wall of his masculine contempt for her sex. Who had taught him not to trust women she wondered and then dismissed the thought as a weakness she shouldn't encourage. She didn't want to know anything about this dark, powerful man. Already he had invaded her life to an extent that made her afraid; the less she knew about him personally, the safer she would be.

'It will be a marriage on paper only,' he replied coolly, 'lasting perhaps only six months if things go according to plan. And as for giving up my freedom ...' His glance mocked her. 'Why on earth should I do that? Unless of course you're trying to tell me that you're prepared to share your body with me as well as your company.'

Colour flared hotly in Cassie's face as she heard his comment. He was making fun of her she thought bitterly. She knew how little he would want a woman like her; a woman who was neither attractive nor witty; a woman who was still really an inexperienced adolescent, far too unattractive to have ever caught his eye, if he hadn't wanted her company.

'I promise you I'd be a far better lover than Peter Williams ...' The soft, dulcet promise behind the words made Cassie's anger burn hotter. He was playing with her, tormenting her all the time knowing that she was the last woman he would want in his bed.

'Technically perhaps,' Cassie agreed, marvelling at the cool derision she had managed to inject into her voice. The look of slight surprise dawning in the dark blue eyes as they studied her gave her the encouragement to go on, 'But I happen to ...'

'Love Williams?' Joel interrupted for her. 'Why? Because he spared you a few kisses and caresses, and for all your brave talk my dear, I doubt it's gone beyond that. You have about you a look of cool purity that I don't believe is assumed. Does the cold virgin you've locked away behind the walls of your intelligence ever rebel, Cassie? Doesn't she ever long to give herself freely and wholeheartedly to the heat of passion?'

His words, edged with scorn as they were, reminded Cassie of all the cruel barbs she had endured as an adolescent, almost without being aware of it she retreated mentally from him, escaping into that small corner of herself she kept hidden from the world. A look of cool dismissal informed the hazel wariness of her eyes, her body composed and outwardly relaxed as she said lightly, 'You're free to make whatever assumptions about me that you wish— just as I'm free not to respond to them. I concede that you've been very clever; that unless I want to destroy everything I've worked for I have to go along with your plans; to agree to this marriage, but I have no intention of living with you as your wife.'

'Not in the fullest sense of the word perhaps,' he agreed, startling her, 'but I certainly intend that our marriage is seen to be completely normal for its brief duration.'

Cassie was stunned enough to demand huskily, 'But why? You can't possibly want . . .'

'What I don't want,' he said ruthlessly cutting off her words, 'is to become the butt of every City joke there is, and if you're wise you'll share my feelings. I'll tell the press that it was a whirlwind romance—they already know I want to take over Cassietronics; romantically inclined as they are it will be an easy step for them to believe our romance began when I approached you with my takeover bid.'

'And in six months' time when the marriage is over?' Why oh why did her voice sound so husky, so hurting somehow, as though already she dreaded the ending that was to come?

'We'll say it didn't work out,' he shrugged. 'We'll face that when we come to it . . .'

'And all your . . .' Cassie's upper lip curled slightly in distaste, 'women friends . . . Will they honestly believe that you preferred a drab little sparrow like me to them?'

'What they believe isn't important,' he told her carelessly, with a monumental display of arrogance. His expression changed as he added curtly, 'You seem to take a perverse delight in running yourself down. Why I wonder? A defensive mechanism perhaps, doing it before anyone else can do it for you?'

He saw too much; came too close to the truth. Desperate to change the subject before he probed any deeper she blurted out, 'And once we are married? Where will we live . . . W . . .'

'*I* shall continue to live in London—I have an apartment there.' He frowned, and Cassie wondered what he was thinking. Of the pleasures he would have to give up for the six months' duration of their marriage? When he next spoke his words shocked her into bitter anger; betraying as they did how far his ideas of how their marriage would work differed from hers.

'I own a house in the Cotswolds—a small estate really. I thought you could live there. There's plenty of space and all the peace and quiet you need to work.'

'In other words, discreetly out of your way,' she said furiously, watching his mouth thin and his eyes harden as he turned towards her.

'What are you trying to say?' he asked her

coldly. 'That you want to share the apartment with me? That you want to share my bed? Was that the price you demanded from Peter Williams for your company? I wonder if Peter was as happy with the bargain as his father? He's known to have a taste for glamorous blondes,' he added cruelly, surveying her with open contempt. 'Hardly your style, but then no doubt his father simply told him to close his eyes and think of Pentatons.'

The sharp sound of her palm connecting with his lean jaw shocked Cassie. She had never hit anyone in anger before in her life, and her face went white as she stared into navy-blue eyes, boring into hers, burning with a heat that made her shiver with fear.

'If you ever do that again, I promise you I'll hit you back,' Joel told her thickly. 'Apart from the fact that you could have caused an accident, I won't tolerate a vitriolic woman.'

'And I won't tolerate being insulted the way you've just insulted me,' Cassie choked back at him. How dare he suggest what he had just suggested? Her body burned with the humiliation of it.

'Why all the emotion?' he queried softly, 'Is it because you think I could be right?'

Cassie didn't deign to answer but sat in icy silence as the powerful car ate up the miles. Inside she was crying out in pain but she would die rather than let Joel Howard see one jot of her anguish. As she stared unseeingly through the windscreen in front of her, only one thought occupied her mind, to the exclusion of all others; and that was a burning desire to make him retract his words; to make him look at her and ache with need for her; and that was surely the most ridiculous, pathetic daydream she had indulged in in all her life; Joel Howard would never, ever want a woman like her.

CHAPTER THREE

THEY reached their destination early in the evening, and Cassie had her first glimpse of Howard Court, just as the late spring sun was setting, bathing the Cotswold stone in a soft rose glow, making the house shimmer like a precious jewel in its rich setting.

When Joel had mentioned an estate she hadn't visualised anything like this. The house wasn't particularly large, but it was old, and very, very gracious, mellowed by time until it blended with the landscape; an inescapable part of a perfect whole.

The house itself was vaguely Elizabethan; green lawns and climbing roses in bud the first things that caught Cassie's eye. It was a dream of a house she thought enviously; it conjured up images of a happy family, of security, love and care. She turned to Joel, too bemused to hold back her pleasure and checked as she saw the dark, almost brooding expression in his eyes. Was he having second thoughts about marrying her? Her heart leapt and it was several seconds before she realised it hadn't jumped in relief.

'It's beautiful,' she said huskily, to cover the shock of her own discovery. 'Have you . . . have you owned it long?'

She was making the natural assumption that he had bought the house with the profits from his successful companies, as so many businessmen did, but his mouth curled sardonically as he responded curtly, 'Personally no, but it's been in my family since the sixteenth century. I inherited it when my father died, a couple of years ago . . .' His face closed up and looked bitter again, and Cassie wondered if perhaps he had been particularly close to the older man and that was why he looked so angry.

'I brought you here so that you could change.' He saw her look of surprise and told her coldly, 'I've arranged for our marriage to be performed by our local vicar. Howards have always married from the village church, and although he accepts that we only want a quiet ceremony—I'm afraid I led him to believe our impatience sprang more from mutual desire than from any practical reasons; he will naturally expect you to look a little bridelike.'

'But I haven't got anything to change into,' Cassie protested.

'That's all taken care of. Come on.' He stopped the car and got out, coming round to her door. No doubt to prevent her from running off Cassie thought bitterly.

Even when he inserted the key into the front door he retained his grip on her arm, his fingers biting into the tender flesh, heating her skin beneath the jacket of her suit. His proximity did strange things to her senses, bemusing them in a way that puzzled and alarmed her. She could smell the male scent of him, warm and faintly musky but instead of being repelled she found it made her want to move closer to him.

Fortunately before she could give in to the alien emotion they were inside the house, stepping on a polished parquet floor.

Motes of dust danced in the air, and she frowned over the hall's look of neglect, wondering how Joel could bear to let this perfect gem of a house look anything less than perfect.

'Upstairs, third on the right,' he told her curtly, 'I'll be waiting outside the door, and there's no 'phone so don't waste your time looking for one. I'll give you fifteen minutes to get ready and if you aren't changed in that time, I'll come in and dress you myself. Understood?'

Yes, Cassie understood all right and she understood too that there would be nothing kind in his hands or touch if he was forced to carry out his threat; rather that it would hold all the cruelty of indifference and distaste, and as she preceded him up the stairs she made a mental vow that she would never, ever give Joel Howard any opportunity to touch her; so that she would never be forced to acknowledge the depth of his contemptuous indifference to her.

The bedroom he had given her faced the back of the house, the windows looking down over an enclosed cobbled courtyard. Urns which had once held flowers stood empty and uncared for, echoing the air of neglect that permeated the whole house. It felt unloved, Cassie thought curiously, and yet if ever a house cried out for love and care it was this one.

She had the impression that Joel almost resented it, and yet if that was the case why keep the estate; why not sell it?

Puzzling over the strange anomalies apparent in his personality she washed quickly in the *en suite* bathroom, emerging dressed in her plain cotton bra and briefs to study the outfit laid out across the bed.

As she looked at it pain and rage mingled in her heart. The dress was a soft creamy white, a confection of delicate lace and fragile silk; a dress designed for a girl like the blonde she had seen Joel dining with or the secretary he had sent to spy on her. Which of them had chosen it, she wondered, acknowledging the cruelty of the mind that had picked such a delicate feminine dress for a woman who had no female graces.

Mindful of Joel's threat she put it on quickly, struggling with the zip which refused to move more than an inch or so above her waist. Temper lent a warm colour to her skin, her hazel eyes more green than golden as she continued to struggle. The silk moulded her body delicately, the ruffles of lace whispering softly as she moved. Some of the pins had escaped from her chignon and strands of hair hung down round her face. Feeling hot and angry she twisted round trying to see what was impeding the closing of the zip. A tiny fragment of fabric seemed to be caught in it, but she could move the fastener neither up nor down and time was running out. A pretty, tiny hat with a provocative veil lay on the bed and she shuddered away from it, all too well able to picture the contrast between that delicately frivolous ornamentation and the heavy frames of her glasses. Impelled by some instinct she couldn't name, she took them off, and stared blearily at her fuzzy reflection. She was just about to put them on when the door opened inward, and Joel strode in. Without her glasses she couldn't see his reflection but she could tell he was angry by the taut way he moved.

'Time's up,' he told her in a clipped voice. He came to a halt just in front of her and for once Cassie was glad of her shortsightedness.

It prevented her from seeing the expression of derision she knew must be in his eyes as he studied her.

'You're not ready,' he said at last. 'Why?'

'The zip's stuck.' Crossly she turned round so that he could see the back of her dress, freezing as she felt the brush of warm fingers against her naked spine. Joel had obviously taken her comment as a request to help her.

His knuckles continued to brush against her skin for what felt like aeons of time. Cassie felt the tiny hairs on her arms stand up as she shivered in reaction to his touch, unaware that she was holding her breath until she felt the zip slide free and she exhaled, making her chest ache.

'All right now?' His voice was derisive and as Cassie searched for her glasses and perched them on the end of her nose she saw that he was watching her with a mingling of contempt and a certain knowing something she couldn't name, but which made her feel increasingly uncomfortable.

'So you do have some female instincts after all,' Joel drawled. Although he had closed her zip his hand still rested on her nape.

'What do you mean?' Cassie was genuinely puzzled, far too thrown off course by his proximity and her own reactions to him to be her normal analytical self.

'I mean, my dear, that it's one of the oldest tricks in the books to invite a man to touch your body under the pretext of needing his help. What

I wonder did women use before the invention of zips?'

As he spoke his fingers were trailing down her spine. 'What exactly was it you wanted from me, Cassie?' he asked her with cold softness. 'This?'

His fingers biting into her collar bone forced her to turn and be taken captive by the hard band of his arms, forcing her along the full length of his body.

She tried to squirm away and could not. Chilled by the taunting 'very proper, and Victorian, but it doesn't alter anything does it?' that Joel murmured against her lips as he brushed them with his.

The impact of his mouth against the sensitive skin of her lips was electrifying, stunning her into frozen stillness.

'Such cool, virginal lips,' Joel drawled, stroking them with his tongue, 'has any man ever turned them to fire, I wonder.' His mouth tugged at her bottom lip, awakening sensations Cassie had never dreamed of experiencing. Her mouth seemed to swell and grow pliantly moist as Joel continued to explore it; coolly and clinically as though he were monitoring an experiment. Reality intruded harshly and Cassie pulled away from him, bitterly angry with herself. How close she had come to melting beneath Joel's mouth; to betraying the yearning need he aroused in her only she knew, and only she *would* know she thought desperately. She couldn't endure the mockery he would exhibit if he knew how close she had been to forgetting why she was in his arms and begging him to kiss her properly. Her face flamed at the narrowness of her escape.

'So you are human after all,' Joel told her indolently, letting her go, 'and it's just a rumour that you've exchanged your emotions for a computer.'

His insult challenged her to respond; not to let him see the devastating effect he had on her. 'I simply wondered what it would be like,' she lied bravely, forcing herself to meet his eyes and to see the narrowed scrutiny with which they explored her.

'Comparing me to Williams you mean?' he invited silkily, and Cassie unaware of the baited trap fell straight into it.

'Yes, that's right,' she agreed eagerly, 'and I much prefer Peter's kisses.' She held her breath, determined to make him believe that a comparison between the two of them was all she had had in mind. Even though she had had no thought in her mind of inviting him to kiss her, she didn't want to tell him that now and risk him questioning why she had allowed him to do so.

'On so short a sampling?' His eyebrows rose. 'You're putting me on my mettle, Cassie, relegating me to second place like that, and without even allowing me to show you what I can really do. You didn't really consider that a kiss did you?' he taunted coming towards her and smiling evilly.

Cassie made to dodge him and cannoned into the foot of the bed, stumbling clumsily. As she fell she lost her glasses and as she bent to retrieve them Joel moved at the same time.

Cassie moaned as she heard glass crunch underfoot. 'What the . . .' Joel swore as he bent down.

'Sorry about that,' he said tersely. He glanced at his watch and frowned. 'We're going to be late.'

'My hair!' Cassie was close to tears. Without her glasses she felt vulnerable and lost. How was she going to tidy her hair if she couldn't see it?

'Leave it down,' Joel advised her, taking matters into his own hands when she objected, and holding her captive as he wrenched the remaining pins out of her hair. Fuzzily Cassie watched him pick up her brush, wincing as he swept it through the tumbled untidyness of her hair.

Her scalp smarted when he had finished and all she could see in the mirror was a pale oval surrounded by a straight dark frame. At least now she couldn't wear the hat, she thought miserably as Joel grasped her arm. Surely no bride had gone to her wedding more ill-prepared. She wasn't wearing a scrap of make-up, not even any lipstick, and she felt ill at ease in her beautiful dress, knowing it could only draw attention to the paucity of her own attractions.

Joel said nothing as he marched her out to the car. It only took ten minutes for him to drive into the village, and park outside the church. No one was about as they walked under the arched gateway and through the graveyard. The door creaked as Joel pushed it open and Cassie froze as she was enveloped in inky blackness, fighting back panic. Another door opened and they were in the church, faint rays of light filtering in through the ornate windows.

'I'm sorry we're a little late.' Joel was apologising to the smiling vicar who approached them. Cassie could tell he was smiling by the tone of his voice.

Joel introduced her and she made some inarticulate response, all too aware of the cruel pressure of Joel's fingers on her hand.

The service was a simple one and in other circumstances could have been indescribably beautiful Cassie thought bleakly. After all what more was needed by two people pledging their lives to one another other than each other, a minister to perform the service and the peace and sanctity that pervaded this small church.

When it was over and Joel's ring weighed heavy and cold on her finger all Cassie could feel was a light-headed sense of relief. She was married to Joel Howard and some tiny part of her took pleasure in that knowledge. Mindful of the impossible dreams of her teenage years Cassie tried to drive the thought away; to deny its existence forcing herself to believe that her relief lay in the fact that the marriage would be a very temporary one. She didn't want to analyse her emotions any further, nor to question why her lips should so clearly remember the touch of Joel's against them. It was dangerous to investigate some things too closely.

She came out of her reverie to hear the vicar saying, 'Mrs Jensen would like you both to have supper with us.'

She saw Joel frown and then heard him agree. 'You'll be making your home down here then?' the vicar asked Joel as they walked from the Church to the vicarage.

'Cassie will certainly live down here,' Joel agreed, glancing in her direction. Cassie couldn't see his expression but she suspected it would be entirely in keeping with that expected of a newly married man, and fear clutched at her heart. He was so adept at concealing his feelings, did anyone ever really know what they were? The depth of her instinctive knowledge about him still had the power to surprise and alarm her, and she was unaware of the tension in her face as they walked into the vicarage, and were introduced to the vicar's wife.

'Cassie is rather shortsighted,' she heard Joel explain on her behalf as she walked into a doorway. 'She didn't want to wear her glasses during the service.'

'You'll have to try contact lenses,' Mrs Jensen told her cheerfully, accepting Joel's statement at face value. 'I find them invaluable. Come and sit down. You must be hungry. Are you going away?' she asked delicately when they were all sitting down and tea had been poured.

'I'm afraid we don't have time right now.' Joel sounded charmingly wry. 'Cassie is working on a new game, and I'm up to my eyes in research. In fact I've got to go back to London tomorrow, unfortunately.' He was looking at her, Cassie knew, but she refused to return his look. Her fingers curled into her palm. Did he really believe he could deceive people into thinking he actually cared about her? The Jensens weren't blind. They could see how plain she was.

'Oh dear,' Mary Jensen sympathised. 'What a shame, but you'll have plenty to occupy yourself with won't you with the house being empty for so long. If you need any help organising a cleaner do let me know. There are several women in the village who'd be glad of the extra money.'

'It's good to have you back, Joel,' she added warmly. 'I know what a blow Andrew's death was to you, and then when your father died we wondered if you might perhaps sell up.'

Waves of bitterness and anger seemed to invade the space between Joel and herself and Cassie turned to him in confused surprise, unable to see his face, but feeling his pain as though it were a tangible thing. Who was Andrew? And why should his death have been a blow to Joel? There was so much about him she didn't know, she thought frustratedly.

'I wanted to, but my father made me promise I wouldn't. Being the younger son I never expected to inherit. I never wanted to inherit. I don't have Andrew's feeling for the land.'

'But you will have children who may inherit it,' Mary Jensen said softly.

Cassie could sense the other woman's sympathy for Joel, just as she could feel his frustrated anger. So Andrew had been Joel's brother. How had he died, she wondered. Had he and Joel not got on; was that the reason for Joel's almost palpable bitterness?

Half an hour later they made their goodbyes, walking in silence back to the parked car.

She wasn't going to be the one to break the silence Cassie told herself firmly, refusing to look at Joel as he started the engine. There were a dozen questions she was dying to ask but she wouldn't utter a single one of them.

Back at the house she followed Joel into a large sitting room attractively furnished in soft blues and yellows. Polished floral cottons covered the settees and chair, the wool carpet soft underfoot. Whoever had furnished the house had good taste and a feel for atmosphere, but the overall impression that Cassie gained was one of sad neglect; as though the house knew of Joel's lack of interest in it and mourned it.

As Cassie sat down she heard Joel pouring himself a drink; a large one by the sound of it, she reflected, marvelling about the power of hearing when it had to take over from sight.

'Would you like a drink?'

She refused his curt offer, staring blindly into the distance, apprehension curling along her spine. They were married. That much had been accomplished. What next?

'I'm returning to London tonight,' Joel told her, answering the most pressing of her questions. 'I can't stop you from carrying out your threat to go to the Press, but think carefully about what you're doing, Cassie. In the long run it would harm us both. Our marriage is a *fait accompli* now.'

'You said you were returning to London,' Cassie responded, marvelling at the calmness of her voice. 'Do I take it that means I'm to remain here?' She wasn't going to tell him yet of her decision to stand by their marriage, although she suspected he had already guessed.

'Yes,' he said curtly. 'There seems little point in your coming back with me to be beseiged by reporters.'

'Yes, I might say the wrong thing mightn't I?' she agreed with fine irony. 'It might have escaped your notice, but I need clothes, Joel, and my spare pair of glasses. After all I can hardly work on the new game if I can't see what I'm doing. I'll also need my small computer,' she added thoughtfully, 'and . . .'

'Write out a list. I'll collect your stuff and bring it down with me when I come back.'

So he *was* planning to come back, Cassie thought wryly. She wasn't to live in total isolation.

A portrait above the fire caught her eye. She could just about make it out, the face familiar enough for her to say, 'Is that you? When . . .'

'Not me,' Joel told her shortly. 'My brother Andrew.'

For a moment Cassie's heart seemed to stop beating. Joel's tone of voice warned her against intruding but she ignored it to say slowly, 'I see . . . You must have been very alike.'

To her surprise Joel laughed harshly, 'In looks yes, in temperament no. Andrew was always a sucker for a sob-story . . . That's what killed him. You want to hear all about it?' He rounded on her and even in spite of her shortsightedness Cassie could clearly see the bitter rage in his eyes. 'All right I'll tell you. He died going after our mother and her lover in an attempt to persuade her to come back to our father. God, I could have told him he was wasting his time. Ten years the affair had been going on. I found out about it when I was at university. I came home unexpectedly one week-end and caught them in bed together; the same bed she had shared with my father . . . but her lover was married too and rather than give up this house and the prestige of being married to my father she kept up the pretence of her marriage and her lover until his wife died and they were able to marry.'

Cassie was left without words. The savagery with which Joel had told his story left her in no doubt as to his bitterness. He must have loved his mother very much at one time, to be so hurt by her defection, she thought sadly. So much about his attitude towards women was now explained.

'Andrew followed them to Italy and was killed in a road accident,' he told her bleakly. 'My father never recovered from that blow. He and Andrew were particularly close.'

Just as Joel and his mother had once been, Cassie thought involuntarily.

'Is your mother . . .'

'I haven't seen her since she left,' Joel told her harshly, 'and nor do I want to see her.'

'I'd better take you upstairs before I leave, I don't want you falling over and breaking your neck.'

'Why not?' she quipped wryly. 'That way you'd get to keep Cassietronics without the burden of having me for a wife . . .'

Across the width of the room, he looked at her. 'What do you want me to say, Cassie?' he asked her expressionlessly. 'That you're not a burden? That I *do* want you?'

Her face flamed at the insolence of his tone. She knew quite well without him having to put it into words that he did not want her.

'You were the one who instigated this marriage, not me, Joel,' she reminded him, chin tilted proudly. 'It might be better if you wrote the list—my handwriting isn't very clear. These are the things I'd like you to bring with you.'

She listed them carefully while he wrote them

down and then accepted his silent escort to the room she had changed in.

She was sitting on the bed when she heard him drive away and a feeling of intense anticlimax washed over her in a wave of depression. What had she expected, she derided herself? That Joel would suddenly succumb to a passionate need of her?

She tried not to think about him as she prepared slowly for bed. She had no night things, and only the underwear which she was wearing which she would have to rinse out to wear tomorrow. She shrugged fatalistically. What did it matter what she wore or didn't wear; she was still totally undesirable.

Towelling herself dry after a quick shower, she automatically avoided her misty reflection in the full length mirror. She hated looking at her body, her skin was too pale, her shape unappealingly slender, her breasts slightly too full to complement the narrowness of her waist and hips. Where was Joel now? Back in London? She must stop thinking about him she told herself shakily. This morning all he had been was a vaguely threatening presence on the outer perimeters of her life; someone from whom she had fled instinctively, fearing his too male aura. Now he was her husband and she was coming closer to understanding her instinctive retreat from him. It humiliated her to admit the desire she felt for him; a desire which was pathetic and undignified and which could never, ever be returned.

The bed felt cold as she slipped into it. Someone must have made it up for her. Joel? Did he expect her to take charge of the house, to run

it as she would do were she really his wife? He
had mentioned that she was working on a new
game to the Jensens; was he hoping to claim the
rights to that game and ultimately to use the
profits it generated for his own companies.
Although he had forced her into marriage he had
said nothing about taking over Cassietronics and
nor would she let him, Cassie decided. The very
fact that they were married should be sufficient
to secure him the financial stability and resources
that he needed to complete his own work. She
would need something to cling to when their
marriage was over, instinct told her that, just as it
told her that no matter how much she denied it
emotionally she was desperately vulnerable to
Joel.

It seemed to be a long time before sleep
claimed her, and when it did she slept only
fitfully, waking periodically, to wonder where she
was and to remember before drifting off again.

'Cassie?'

The coolly commanding tone of the male voice
intruding on her dreams was familiar. Reluctantly
Cassie opened her eyes, blinking at the strong
sunlight filling the room. She was lying on her
stomach, her face buried in her pillow. The voice
came from behind her and she rolled over
automatically turning towards it, disturbing her
covers as she did so. It wasn't until she felt the
cool, fresh air from the open window slide over
her skin that she remembered her nudity and by
then it was too late to prevent Joel's thorough
scrutiny of her bare shoulders and breasts.

Thankful that she couldn't see his expression,
Cassie reached shakily for the sheet, recoiling as

though she had been burned when his fingers brushed against hers.

'Such modesty,' he drawled softly, watching the colour stain her skin. He retained his grip of the sheet, and Cassie was burningly aware of his fingers resting against the upper swell of her breast.

'Who would have thought you were so femininely shaped beneath those drab garments you seem to favour?'

Cassie couldn't bear to look at him as she heard his mocking taunt. He seemed to enjoy hurting her. She knew quite well how he must view her body when he compared it to those of his other women.

'Don't . . .' the protest was uttered before she could silence it, her voice thick with anguish and shame. She thought his eyebrows drew together frowningly as she struggled to make out his expression, longing for the protection of her clothes.

'Don't what?' he demanded softly, and it seemed to Cassie that he was watching her quite intently. 'Don't tell you that you have an attractive body?'

Her moan of protest was completely instinctive, but it seemed to have an odd effect on Joel. Instead of laughing at her, he said tautly, 'What is it, Cassie? Aren't I allowed to comment on my wife's sexuality? Is that privilege reserved for Williams? Is that it?'

Cassie fought to understand what he was saying, her forehead furrowing.

'Nothing to say?'

The fingers that had been resting against her

skin curled round the sheet, yanking it down to
her waist before she could stop him. She reacted
instinctively, reaching blindly for it and trying to
pull it up again.

'Stop!' Joel's curt command stilled her frantic
movements. 'You're my wife. Surely I can look at
you if I wish?'

Cassie felt the bed depress under his weight as
he sat down on it. His hand seemed to burn into
the skin of her waist as he held the sheet against
her there. He was close enough to her for her just
to be able to make out his features. His eyes
seemed a darker, deeper blue than she remembered, his facial bones tighter, his mouth
surprisingly, not hard, but curved into a line of
sensual warmth.

'Please leave me alone and go away.' Cassie
blurted out the plea, as she tried to control the
tremors invading her body.

'In a minute. Right now I feel more like kissing
my new wife.'

'No.' The word exploded into the air between
them.

'Why not?' His voice was deceptively casual.
'Last night you were only too eager to be kissed;
to compare me with Peter Williams.'

He was leaning towards her and Cassie felt the
breath stifle in her throat. He had not the
slightest desire to kiss her really she knew that,
but beneath the suave smile he was giving her she
sensed a deep vein of burning anger; a force too
great to be contained, demanding expression in
an explosion of violence and for some reason he
was directing that violence towards her. Tears
stung the back of her throat. Why was he

tormenting her like this? Did he really loathe her so much?

Numbly she watched his hands move, slowly cupping her breasts, his thumbs stroking their tender crests. His touch was light and gentle but Cassie still shivered beneath it, her tremors increasing as she gradually became aware of the feelings his touch was arousing inside her. Part of her wanted to melt; to dissolve beneath the sweet torment of his touch; to yield herself completely in a way that was entirely instinctive, but her mind urged caution warning her that she was being used; that Joel was playing some demoniacal game of his own and that she could only be hurt if she joined in it.

With a tremendous effort of will Cassie averted her eyes from the sight of Joel's hands on her body, fighting to control her racing heart and deny the prickles of awareness sensitising her skin.

'Have you seen the Press?'

Her voice seemed to come from far away, weak and thickly husky.

'Yes.' The cool emotionless affirmative was uttered without him ceasing stroking her skin. Beneath the delicate caresses Cassie could feel her nipples hardening, burgeoning like delicate flowers opening to the sun.

'So you *are* female after all.'

The mocking words cut into her skin like lashes, burning her with pain. She wanted to struggle but sensed dimly that for some reason Joel wanted her to do just that.

'Why are you doing this?' she asked him numbly, unable to choke back the pain-filled demand.

'You're my wife, and since my girlfriend tells me that she is not prepared to share my bed as long as I remain married to you it seems only fair that you should take her place, wouldn't you say?'

Several facts struck Cassie at the same time. Firstly, and somehow most painfully, he must have gone straight from her to the blonde woman she had seen him with in the restaurant. Secondly, he was furiously, bitterly angry at his girlfriend's defection, and Cassie no longer wondered about the source of the chained violence she had sensed in him the moment he touched her.

'This wasn't part of our agreement,' she told him quietly, 'and I don't want this from you, Joel.'

For a moment he seemed surprised; then she saw the speculation darken his eyes as she forced herself to meet them.

'I could make you want it,' he threatened softly. The pads of his thumbs lingered on the hard nubs of her breasts and for one crazy moment Cassie was tempted to encourage him, to push him into making good his threat. After all she was human wasn't she? Just as capable of experiencing desire and need as any more attractive woman. Just because she was plain it didn't mean she couldn't feel . . . what? Desire? A need to be convinced that she was desirable? Capable of arousing a man? Brought abruptly down to earth Cassie shuddered deeply. What was she thinking of? Joel didn't desire her. He was motivated purely by a need to punish her sex. The narrowness of her escape shocked her. She had been within a heartbeat of begging him to make love to her. The humiliation of this admission made her skin sting with hot colour, the heat that had previously infiltrated her veins, heating her body into languorous desire, draining away and leaving in its place a sick self-disgust.

'You mean you could make my body want it,' she told Joel dully, 'but I won't be used to assuage your need for another woman, Joel.' She faced him squarely, forcing herself to overcome her embarrassment at her nudity. Now that she looked at him properly she could see tiredness and disillusionment clearly outlined on his face. His glance glittered briefly over her body and then returned to meet hers.

'Very well, my cold little virgin wife,' he taunted curtly, 'but first perhaps you ought to have a little taste of what you're refusing.'

He had pinned her back against the bed before she could move, the faintly rough fabric of his casual wool shirt rubbing against her breasts, the full weight of his body hard against hers, as his fingers curled into her hair and tightened almost painfully, forcing her to lie unmoving, unable to turn her head to avoid the downward descent of his head. She watched his mouth coming nearer, her heart thudding heavily, her breathing constricted. Without her being aware of it her lips parted and quivered tensely. A dark flush stained Joel's cheekbones, his eyes glittering febrilely.

This time there was no lightly persuasive strokes of his lips and tongue against her mouth, just a hungry, angry pressure as it slanted across hers, enveloping her in a fiercely sexual tide of mingled rage and need.

When she refused to open her mouth his teeth

nipped painfully at her bottom lip, his tongue savouring the small drop of blood that welled from the wound the moment after her inarticulate cry of pain forced her lips to part.

Cassie fought the domination of his kiss instinctively and fiercely, arching her back in an attempt to dislodge his weight from her body, but all he did was tangle his fingers more painfully into her hair, holding her head rigid as he released one hand and used it to grip her waist as she arched, forcing her against the hard length of his body.

Only when he had finally subdued her, did the fierce pressure of his mouth relent a little, his tongue caressing the swollen soreness of her bottom lip, his hands leaving her hair to stroke slowly down her body.

During their struggles several buttons of his shirt had come undone and Cassie flinched back automatically from the rough contact of his body hair against the tender peaks of her breasts.

'For such a slim little thing you have a surprisingly voluptuous body.'

The husky words made her tense, her eyes opening to meet what she felt sure would be the taunting mockery of Joel's. Instead his eyes were a deeply dense blue, his mouth hovering over hers as he breathed the words into her.

'Your breasts fit perfectly into my hands,' he told her, demonstrating the truth of his words.

Cassie shuddered, feeling her body's instant response, knowing she was quivering in reaction to the slow circles Joel was drawing round her nipples and unable to do a thing about it. He was teaching her body patterns of response it would remember until she drew her last breath, she thought achingly. He moved and she felt the rough abrasion of the dark hairs covering his chest scrape arousingly against her skin. It was an effort to draw breath into her taut lungs and when Joel bent his head towards the soft swell of her breast Cassie could only watch him torn between longing and despair.

She made a sound in her throat a soft groan that seemed to drain the tension out of Joel. He looked at her and smiled, a cold, mocking smile that made her want to cry out in acute pain.

'There,' he said softly, as he released her. 'That's something for you to think about the next time you start comparing me with Peter Williams.'

She turned her head away as he left her room, she was overcome with a mixture of humiliation and self-contempt. What was he doing to her? Shaking her head Cassie pulled back the bedcovers and ran into her bathroom, quickly locking the door and turning on the shower, wanting to punish her body with the sting of cold water, for its betrayal.

Joel wasn't by nature a sadistic man; instinct told her that, and yet he was showing towards her a streak of cruelty that seemed to have no logic to it. He had chosen to marry her of his own free will. She had known he didn't desire her as a proper wife without him having to reinforce that lesson. Had his behaviour sprung entirely from his quarrel with his girlfriend? Could frustration drive a man to the point where he would behave as Joel had behaved towards her this morning? He was an attractive virile man, and an extremely

wealthy one, Cassie couldn't imagine that he
would have the slightest trouble in finding a
replacement for his blonde playmate. He couldn't
have been in love with her. She didn't know how
she knew that, but she did know it. Joel Howard
would never allow himself to be vulnerable
enough to any woman to fall in love. He hated
and despised her sex Cassie thought as she
towelled herself dry, punishing them all perhaps
for his mother's failings?

And yet there had been one moment when he
touched her when she had sensed in him a
purely masculine need to subdue her, to make
her want him and respond to him. She had
been imagining things, Cassie told herself
bitterly. Why on earth should a man like Joel
Howard want a woman like her; a woman
who he knew no other man had ever wanted.
That knowledge had been there in his mocking
description of her as a virgin.

She had rubbed her skin until it glowed, too
engrossed in what she was doing to stop, but now
as she let the towel drop and remembered that
her clothes were in the bedroom Cassie forced
herself to study the full-length reflection of her
nude body, she could see in the bathroom's floor
to ceiling mirror.

Voluptuous Joel had said, and Cassie shuddered as she studied her breasts, full and gently
rounded, different now somehow. Just for a
moment she was overwhelmed with an intense
need to punish him for what he had made her
realise about herself and her sexuality; and the
best punishment would be to make him want her
as she had wanted him, to torment him and make

him suffer the same humiliation she had had to endure; that of knowing herself aroused by someone who had not the slightest desire for her. Grimacing at herself she unlocked the bedroom door. Joel must have been back while she was in the bathroom because her suitcase lay on the floor. She must be mad to even dream that she could make Joel want her she told herself as she took out clean underclothes, frowning slightly over their serviceable plainness for the first time in her life, sparing more than a brief glance for the sensible white cotton. No doubt Joel's women adorned themselves in silk and lace . . . Pushing aside a too vivid image of his blonde girlfriend adorned in just such articles Cassie concentrated on getting dressed.

As she made her way downstairs she heard a 'phone ring. It was answered quickly, no doubt by Joel. One door in the hallway stood slightly open and Cassie headed towards it automatically, no thought of eavesdropping in her mind until she heard Joel saying angrily, 'And I've told you, Fiona, my marriage stands.' There was a tense silence and then he spoke again. 'My reasons for marrying are none of your business.'

So he hadn't told his girlfriend the truth, Cassie reflected as she moved away in the direction of the kitchen. Suddenly for no good reason she felt a spear of tremulous excitement pierce through her, swiftly stilled as her mind challenged her heart. 'Do you think he could ever really want you?' it demanded mockingly. Surely she had learned in her teens just how unattractive she was to men, Cassie asked herself as she started to make some coffee. Surely she wasn't stupid enough to indulge in impossible daydreams of Joel Howard? He would never look at her with desire in his eyes; never want her as he had made her want him, and she might as well accept that fact.

CHAPTER FOUR

THAT morning the 'phone barely stopped ringing. When it came to getting the right sort of publicity Joel was a genius Cassie reflected wryly, watching him answer it for the umpteenth time and give the listening reporter the by now familiar story about how they had met and fallen in love.

Listening to him and imagining how it might have been were his fabrications true Cassie felt the stirrings of an idea deep inside her. A mirthless laugh trembled on her still faintly swollen lips. How ironic it would be if the idea she could feel taking form in her mind right now should turn out to be her most successful game. It would be a challenge to chart the course of a game through the hazards of falling in love. Leaving Joel to his telephone calls she went upstairs to her room and started making notes.

'Cassie?'

The curt inflection of Joel's voice brought her back to reality. 'There's no point in sulking up here,' he continued brusquely. 'We might be invaded by the Press this afternoon. Remember you're supposed to be a glowingly happy bride.'

'Whose bridegroom couldn't even be bothered to take her away on honeymoon,' she queried lightly. 'What will the Press make of that do you suppose?'

'They'll make of it what they're told. Namely that business commitments prevent us from getting away right now but that later I'll be taking you away somewhere suitably romantic.' He saw the colour leave her face and added tauntingly, 'How does that appeal to your logical mind, Cassie? Would you, do you suppose, succumb to the lure of a tropical island paradise?'

'I've always believed that when one is truly in love and loved in return, surroundings aren't important,' she told him coolly, hoping he wouldn't notice the betraying thud of her heart.

'How romantic—and how unexpected.' His eyes narrowed challengingly. 'Tell me, Cassie, have you ever been in love ... and loved in return?'

Oh how she longed for the face-saving ability to lie, but she couldn't, her baldly unequivocal 'No,' falling into the tense silence of her room.

'Your logical little mind wouldn't let you I suppose.'

Cassie gripped her fingers into tightly balled fists, almost hating him for tormenting her in this way. He must know how slender the possibility was of anyone falling in love with her. She was too plain; too dull and far, far too clever. She had learned that much at school and had those lessons reinforced by her father, who had warned her that she would have to be able to make her own way through life; that she would have to be independent.

'As I have to spend the next six months in this house, I'd like your permission to hire someone to help me to clean it,' Cassie told him, completely changing the subject and turning away from him so that he wouldn't be able to read in her face how much she was already entranced by the house, and how she longed with every deeply feminine instinct she possessed to turn it back into the home she sensed it had once been.

Anger, and bitter pain clashed in his eyes for a moment before he replied and Cassie thought he was going to refuse, but in the end he simply said tersely, 'Organise whatever you like. I should have got rid of this place when I inherited it, but I promised my father I wouldn't.'

'It's beautiful and yet you seem to hate it,' Cassie murmured bravely, wondering how he would react to her words. He was a man who deeply resented any attempts to get close to him, she had discovered that, and she doubted that even his girlfriends knew more about him than he wanted them to know.

'I grew up knowing that Andrew would inherit it. When you can't have something or someone you love you have to put up barriers against wanting them or endure agonising pain.' He wasn't really seeing her Cassie realised, but talking almost to himself, looking back into the past, his voice suddenly harsh as he added. 'When I look at this house I can't help remembering how I came by it . . .'

'You must have loved your brother very much.' She said it with soft sympathy, unprepared for the bitter, dark glitter that entered his eyes.

'As a child there were times when I hated him—hated him for being the elder, for being our mother's favourite. Now do you understand why I loathe this place? Every time I look at it I remember all the times as a child when I wished

Andrew unborn.' His mouth twisted bitterly, the mask of indifferent contempt he habitually wore slipping back into place, his eyes shuttered, as though he resented her for letting him betray such intensely personal emotions.

As an only child, Cassie didn't know what to say; she knew that sibling rivalry was a common affliction of childhood, but sensed that to say as much to Joel would only draw his contemptuous bitterness down on her head.

'In my mother's time every room in the house seemed to be full of flowers, laughter and sunshine. Andrew and I were away at school and I used to long to come back. That was before I discovered it was all a sham; that my mother had a lover.'

Remembering that he had said he had found them in bed together and that his mother was responsible for his brother's death Cassie kept quiet.

'Have you anything better to wear than that?' Joel asked abruptly grimacing disdainfully at her dull beige skirt and matching blouse. 'We're supposed to be newly married remember? If the Press do arrive they'll expect to find you radiant; dressed to please your bridegroom.'

'I'm so sorry you don't approve of my clothes,' Cassie retorted, angered by his contempt. 'Unfortunately they weren't chosen with you in mind.'

'Me or any other man,' he agreed tautly. 'My God, why do you insist on covering yourself in these drab garments?' His fingers flicked at the unflattering fullness of her skirt, chosen because Cassie believed it concealed the narrowness of her hips, so disproportionate in her view to the full curves of her breasts. 'They make you look . . .'

'Even plainer than I already am?' she challenged bitterly. 'I realise that I don't measure up to your usual standards of female pulchritude, but you should have considered that when you forced me into this marriage,' she flung at him.

'What are you trying to prove?' he demanded, his mouth twisting sardonically. 'That brains are just as exciting as beauty? You were engaged to Peter Williams. What did you and he do when you were alone? Exchange computer data?'

It was so near the truth that Cassie almost hated him, but his mention of Peter reminded her that she still had the latter's ring. That would have to be returned, and she would have to write to Peter in explanation. What explanation she asked herself, sighing as she realised that she would have to pretend to him that she and Joel were deeply in love. Faint colour stung her skin as she remembered the looks Peter had cast her occasionally when he thought she wasn't looking; distasteful, resigned looks. Like Joel, Peter favoured pretty, feminine blondes.

'Now what are you thinking?'

'I'm thinking about Peter,' Cassie replied. 'I'll have to get in touch with him, explain . . .'

'That I coerced you into marriage to prevent his father from getting his hands on your company. Oh no. When you see or talk to Peter Williams, I fully intend to be there. You persist in seeing him as your white knight, don't you, Cassie? But in reality he was going to sell you down the river. His father had already picked out the executive who was going to take over your company.'

'No.' Cassie's denial was a sharp exclamation of pain. 'No, I was going to retain full control.'

Joel's smile was taunting. 'You *are* living in cloud cuckoo land aren't you? Ralph Williams was desperate to get control of your company, and there was no way he was going to allow you to remain in control.'

'As desperate as you?' Cassie challenged quickly. 'At least as Peter's wife I would have had a proper husband . . .'

The moment the reckless words were uttered Cassie regretted them. Lean fingers gripped her wrist, exerting almost bruising pressure, an expression of anger so intense tightening Joel's facebones that she flinched. 'And you wanted that so desperately that you were prepared to buy him?' he demanded through closed teeth. 'Where's your pride, Cassie? Surely you think more of yourself than to . . .' He broke off and swore, startling her with his vehemence. For a moment she had almost believed that he considered she was too good for Peter Williams. Her imagination playing tricks on her again she thought tiredly as he released her, frowning over the renewed ring of the telephone.

Later that afternoon, as Joel had prophesied they received a visit from the Press. Cassie hated posing for the photograph they requested. Even the popular non-financial press were represented. Their romance would make a good public interest story, they told Cassie who was mentally flinching away from their curiosity, feeling sure that they must be doubting that Joel could ever have fallen in love with someone like her.

One of the reporters might almost have picked up on her train of thought, Cassie thought moments later as he questioned, 'Surely, Mr Howard, you'll benefit doubly from this marriage? With a successful company like Cassietronics brought under your umbrella, your investors will have renewed faith in you.'

'That's quite true,' Joel agreed with a brief smile, 'but there is one reason and one reason alone why I married my wife, and she knows what that is.' He turned to Cassie and picked up her hand, conveying her tense fingers to his lips. Anger and desire fought a tumultuous battle inside her as spears of pleasure shot along her veins from her fingertips. Joel had no right to use her in this way her mind cried out in protest; he was deliberately and callously exerting the sensual pressure he knew she was vulnerable to, using her vulnerability for his own purposes.

When the reporters had gone, Cassie felt limp and exhausted. So much in her life had changed in such a short space of time. It shocked her to hear Joel saying that he had already made arrangements to re-let the lease of her flat. 'For six months only of course ... I'm going back to London tonight, I'll clear the rest of your stuff out tomorrow and bring it down here.'

'I'd prefer to do that myself,' Cassie told him coldly.

'Oh no, you're staying here, where I can keep an eye on you ...'

'Living the life of a nun,' Cassie said bitterly. 'While you lead one as a bachelor in London. I hope whoever you're seeing tonight is more understanding of your married status than the one you saw last night.

His cruel, 'Careful, you're beginning to sound like a real wife,' hurt her. 'Surely you can't be jealous, my heart's darling?' he added tauntingly.

'Jealous?' Cassie forced herself to sound uncaring. 'No one with any sense would be jealous of the purely physical involvement you have with your women, Joel. I don't believe you're capable of any real emotion.'

She held her breath as she watched him, knowing the unconsidered words were true and wondering how he would react to them. Strangely enough after an initial tightening of his mouth all he said was, 'Your innocence is showing, Cassie. Physical satisfaction can be a lot more pleasurable than emotional trauma. Don't wait up for me,' he added tormentingly as he sauntered out of the room.

It was an hour later when he left. Going upstairs on her way to her room as he drove away Cassie caught the faint scent of his cologne, spicy and masculine. His room was opposite hers and she lingered by the door, hesitating before giving in to the temptation to push it open.

His room was the same size as hers, but furnished so spartanly it might almost have been the cell of a monk. The large bed was covered in a dark brown spread. The walls were bare, the carpet plain. It was a coldly austere room, an empty room, she thought wonderingly, the room of a man who suffered torments other people knew nothing about.

'Looking for something?' The smoky voice behind her made her jump guiltily, bright patches of colour staining her face as she swung round and saw Joel standing behind her, hands in his pockets as he surveyed her with mocking amusement.

She hadn't heard him come back, and for a brief moment thought perhaps he had changed his mind about going out. 'I forgot this,' he told her shattering her daydream as he picked up a leather blouson jacket from a chair.

Long after he had gone Cassie's skin burned from the humiliation of being discovered standing gazing at his room like a moon-struck teenager. He aroused emotions inside her she couldn't analyse; emotions which ranged from a fiercely bitter resentment, to an almost maternal compassion. No one had ever touched so many chords inside her so deeply in her life, and she wished with all her heart that Joel Howard had not been the one to do so.

Joel hadn't returned in the morning by the time she had finished breakfast and so Cassie decided to walk down to the Vicarage and take Mrs Jensen up on her offer of help.

She found the vicar's wife in her garden. She smiled warmly at Cassie and said teasingly, 'No bridegroom this morning?'

'Joel had to go to London last night—on business,' Cassie told her, hoping she wasn't colouring up. 'I came to see you about getting some help in the house. It looks so sad and neglected at the moment.'

'Yes, it's a house that responds well to a woman's love and care,' Mrs Jensen agreed, looking shrewdly at Cassie. 'I'm glad Joel didn't sell it. I sometimes think he's torn between loving it and hating it.'

'He feels guilty about inheriting it,' Cassie told her, feeling sure that the vicar's wife had already guessed this. 'Deep down inside I think he does love it.'

'Yes, so do I. As a child he always felt things far more deeply than Andrew. Andrew was his father all over again, stoical, not very imaginative, a kind man, but not one who could ever really stir a woman's passions.' She glanced thoughtfully at Cassie. 'Has Joel told you about his mother?'

'He told me that she left his father,' Cassie said carefully.

'Yes, poor Miranda.' Her sympathy for Joel's mother caught Cassie off-guard. She would have expected the other woman to be more disapproving.

'She should never have married Gerald, but her grandmother pushed her into it. She was orphaned during the war, and her grandmother had old-fashioned ideas. Gerald was ten years older than Miranda when they married, and already settled into middle age. Some men are like that aren't they? Miranda was only eighteen, a bright lively girl.' She sighed. 'I was one of her bridesmaids. She and I were at school together. It was through her that I met Tom. At first she was happy enough with the house, and then the children when they came along, but she had gone straight from school into marriage, she hadn't really lived and she was a woman who cried out for life,' Mrs Jensen told Cassie softly. 'She was so pretty; so vividly alive, and very, very popular.

She met Nico when he came over here on business. At first she fought terribly hard against the attraction, but she got no support from Gerald; he never really treated her like a desirable woman. She was his wife, the mother of his sons, and that was all there was to it. I couldn't blame her when she left him. Really they should never have married.'

'Joel feels terribly bitter about her,' Cassie said quietly.

Mrs Jensen sighed again. 'Yes, I know, poor boy. He adored her . . .'

'And she preferred Andrew.'

Mrs Jensen looked surprised. 'Good heavens, what on earth gave you that idea, Joel was always her favourite. I remember when he was a baby she used to spend hours playing with him. Andrew was his father's son, but Joel was hers. Of course she knew that she would never be allowed to keep them if she and Gerald divorced. In those days divorce wasn't like it is today, and although she never discussed it with me I could see how torn she was; Nico or the children. Then Gerald sent the boys off to school when Andrew was ten and Joel eight. I think it was from then that she started to distance herself from Joel, knowing that she was going to leave.'

'But Joel was twenty before his parents were divorced?' Cassie protested.

Mrs Jensen looked extremely unhappy. 'Even though Gerald didn't really love her, Miranda was his wife; when she told him she wanted a divorce he was bitterly angry. She came to me in a dreadful state.' The older woman bit her lip. 'There was a bruise on her face. She told me she

fell as she left the house, but I've always believed
that Gerald hit her. If she hadn't been so
overwrought I doubt she'd have told me as much
as she did, but she was so distressed that it all
came out. Gerald had threatened to deny that
Joel was his child if she tried to get a divorce.'

She saw Cassie pale and nodded grimly, 'Yes
you can imagine what that did to Miranda. "I
only wish he *was* Nico's," she told me, "and even
though he isn't, Nico would welcome him as his
son, but I can't do that to him, I can't let him
grow up eternally wondering who his father is, I
can't do it Mary".'

'So she stayed with her husband until Joel
discovered about Nico and his father was forced
to face up to the situation?' Cassie said quietly.

'So she stayed,' Mary Jensen agreed quietly.
'Sacrificing her own happiness for Joel's peace of
mind, and for her pains earning his hatred.'

Tears stung Cassie's eyes. She longed to go to
Joel and tell him what she had just heard, but she
knew that even if she could persuade him to listen
he wouldn't believe her, and yet if he was able to
believe it, it would ease so much of the burden of
pain he carried around with him.

Why should she care about his pain Cassie
asked herself as she walked back to the house.
What had he ever done to earn her compassion,
her . . . concern? Nothing. She was becoming too
involved with him; and that involvement was all
on her side. He didn't care a single jot about her.
He was just using her, and she would do well to
bear that fact in mind.

CHAPTER FIVE

JOEL had been gone for three days, and Cassie, in his absence, had run the full gamut of emotions from anger through to exhausted depression. She shivered as she contemplated the cold vastness of the large kitchen, wishing that she knew how to activate the central heating system. The weather had suddenly turned cold and the few clothes Joel had brought her from her flat did not include anything warm enough for the present low temperatures.

The only bright spot in her life was the new game she was working on. Her own emotional responsiveness to Joel and the resentment it sparked off inside her had made her bubble with ideas, rather in the same way that her temper simmered just below the boiling mark, she thought wryly as she plugged in the coffee machine and started to make herself a drink.

The few supplies Joel had got in were running low, so she would have to walk to the village to get some more. It struck her, almost immediately that she had next to no money with her. Fortunately she did have her cheque book, but did the village possess a bank?

Another visit to Mary Jensen was called for. Mary had rung her the previous day inviting her to call anyway. It seemed that she had found her some help for the house.

Cassie had now fully explored her new home. It

had been decorated with excellent taste and a verve that was still as fresh today as it had been when Joel's mother had decorated it, so that very little needed to be done apart from organising a thorough cleaning of the carpets and curtains and a freshening up of the paintwork.

The kitchen was the only room that needed much attention. In Cassie's view it needed completely reorganising, new units, new equipment, everything, but she wanted to talk to Joel before she involved herself in anything so drastic. After all, she would only be staying here a matter of months; it wasn't really her home, only a temporary habitation. A sense of acute desolation enveloped her. Already the house had come to mean something to her. It reached out and warmed her in a way that her own flat had never done. Not normally given to emotional reactions Cassie was acutely aware of the lingering warmth of Joel's mother in almost every room. She could sense the sympathy and vibrancy of the other woman's personality almost as a physical reality, a comforting sensation of not being completely alone.

Once she had made her coffee Cassie made her way to the small library she had made her work base. Her new game involved a series of complicated moves which ultimately would lead to an appropriately happy-ever-after ending to the romantic chase nature of the game. She felt it would have considerable appeal for women, and already was beginning to feel quite excited about its potential.

It was only when she was working that she was fully able to blot out those moments in Joel's arms; to dismiss the spine-tingling sensations his touch had aroused in her and the knowledge that she had wanted him to go on, to make love to her as though he did actually desire her. It was a humiliating thought to admit. Long, long ago she had forced herself to see herself as she really was, unclouded by the mists of wishful thinking; she was a plain, dull girl, with an excellent brain who did not have the looks or the personality to attract men. She had already decided that this was their loss rather than hers; that if they preferred sugary sweetness then so be it; she wasn't going to waste tears over that fact, but suddenly she found herself longing as never before for the glamour she realised she had been denied in her early teens.

Joel had brought her spare pair of glasses which were even more unflattering than the ones he had broken. Their heaviness seemed to crush the fragile bone structure of Cassie's face, although when she glanced in the mirror all she saw was a too pale, too small face that seemed to have no colour or prettiness to it whatsoever.

Had Joel's girlfriend had a change of heart, she wondered—losing her concentration as the unwanted thought intruded. But then what did it matter if she had not. Joel had made it clear that there were others more than willing to step into the shoes she had vacated, and Cassie had no difficulty in believing that.

Were they as aware of his contempt of their sex as she was she pondered, or did their own self-confidence in their attractiveness blunt their awareness of the finely tuned contempt she had seen so clearly?

What would Joel do, she wondered, if she were
to contact the Press, to tell them what he had
done. She looked at the 'phone and was just
reaching for it when she remembered his
warning. He was right; she would lose all her own
credibility if she made public the truth, and she
couldn't afford to take that risk. She was involved
in a highly competitive field, of which at the
moment she was the leader, but there was an
eager pack behind her, all of whom would be only
too willing to take her place were she to falter.

Sighing she turned her attention back to her
game. She was growing colder and colder, and
she almost yielded to the temptation to ring Joel
up and ask him how she could start the central
heating. Pride made her stop. She could just
picture Joel's expression were she to telephone
him. No doubt he was used to women ringing
him on all manner of pretexts and with his male
logic he would assume she was simply another.
Dimly she sensed a streak of cruelty in him that
would exploit any weakness he found in her,
purely because she was female. Her weakness was
her unexpected reaction to him; the sexual
chemistry he sparked off inside her body that
made her aware of herself; her desires and needs,
in a way she had never known before. He would
subjugate her if he could, by whatever means he
could, Cassie acknowledged. The need to do so
was a legacy left by what he considered his
mother's betrayal. Sighing she resigned herself to
the increasing coldness, until she remembered the
immersion heater that warmed the water. A hot
bath would warm her chilled body, and then
perhaps a brisk walk down to the vicarage. Mrs

Jensen might know something about the intricacies of the central heating system, whose control panel totally baffled Cassie.

She was just drying herself when she heard the sound of a car outside. Unable to see who it was through the opaque window of her bathroom, she hurriedly pulled on a robe, and opened the bathroom door, hurrying through her bedroom.

Her hair was damp at the ends where it had escaped from her shower cap, and had started to curl slightly, her skin flushed from the heat of the water, but Cassie was oblivious to these things, having forgotten in her haste to put on her glasses.

The first thing she felt as she tugged open the door was a plunging sense of disappointment. The second was astonishment, because it wasn't Joel standing outside the door as she had hoped, but Peter Williams.

Without her glasses Cassie could not make out his expression and so was unaware of his narrowed, startled assessment of her as he took in the slender length of her legs beneath the hem of her robe, the attractive disorder of her hair, and the warm flush colouring her skin.

'Peter!'

Her evident astonishment made him frown in irritation.

'Don't sound so surprised,' he advised her bitterly. 'Remember, until a handful of days ago, we were engaged.'

'You got my letter?'

'Only after I'd read about the wedding in the papers,' he told her bitterly. 'Cassie, what's happened? My parents couldn't believe it and neither could I. I thought you hated Howard, or was that just a double game you were playing, lulling us into a false sense of security while all the time . . .'

The expression on her face checked him, and he suppressed the remainder of what he had been going to say with an effort. He had never particularly wanted to marry her, but his father had been insistent, and yet when he discovered that Joel Howard had snatched her from underneath his nose, he had felt acutely resentful. Howard was welcome to her he had told his father savagely, when the latter had berated him for letting her slip through their fingers, and yet now, seeing her looking so unexpectedly feminine and vulnerable his pulse rate quickened, his rage against Joel Howard deepening. Shallow minded at the best of times, it took him only seconds to persuade himself that he had genuinely cared about Cassie and that Joel Howard had robbed him of a much-desired bride as well as a potential fortune.

'Aren't you going to ask me in?' His eyes assessed the soft curves of Cassie's breasts beneath the towelling robe. He had always considered her a frigid little thing, but suddenly he wasn't so sure.

'Why did you do it, Cass?' he asked softly when Cassie had led him into the library.

Almost, Cassie was tempted to tell him the truth, and then she remembered what Joel had said about his father's plans for her company. She had never deceived herself about Peter's feelings for her or hers for him, but she had expected both he and his father to stick by their word that she would remain in charge of Cassietronics.

'It just happened,' she murmured vaguely, her forehead furrowing as she asked slowly. 'Peter, if we had married, what would have happened to Cassietronics if I had had a child?'

Peter frowned, obviously not following her train of thought. 'Dad had all that sorted out, Cassie. He had hand-picked one of his best men, Andrew Kershaw, to run Cassietronics for you. Neither of us wanted you to have to cope with the double burden of being a wife and mother and struggling to run the company as well.'

It sounded so reasonable and well meaning, but Cassie wasn't deceived, Joel had been right, she thought wryly. Even though she couldn't see Peter's expression she could sense his restlessness.

'How did it just happen, Cass?' he persisted. Dark colour stormed up over his skin as a possibility suddenly struck him. 'Did he seduce you?' he demanded hoarsely. 'Is that what happened, Cass? Did he put you in a position where he felt you had to marry him?'

Peter was half right, Cassie thought; Joel certainly had put her in a position where she couldn't refuse him, but not by seducing her. She could just make out the angry colour darkening Peter's normally pale skin and wondered a little at it, before caution urged her not to let him leave without setting the record straight. It would not do her reputation in the business world any good if Peter started spreading the rumour that Joel had seduced her, and something told her that he probably would.

'Don't be silly, Peter,' she responded coolly.
'I'm not some Victorian virgin you know. No
woman in the nineteen-eighties needs to marry
simply because she's lost her virginity.'

'But you did sleep with him before you were
married?' he almost snarled, his vehemence
surprising her. 'All the time I was playing the
good little fiancé, letting you hold me off with all
that coy coldness, you were sneaking into his bed,
is that it?'

His reaction was not at all what Cassie had
expected. Half amused she assimilated the
information that Peter, simply because he now
believed that she and Joel had been lovers, had
persuaded himself that he too had wanted her,
when she knew that he had not.

'I don't want to talk about it any more,' she told
him crisply, 'Joel and I are married, Peter. I'm
sorry if you don't think I played fair with you . . .'

'Played fair—you were *engaged* to me dammit!'
he swore at her coming towards her. 'I suppose
Howard put you up to that. He knew how
desperately . . .' He broke off plainly angry with
himself for saying too much.

'Your father needed my company?' Cassie
supplied directly. 'Yes, I'm afraid he did.'

Once she was free of this fake marriage to Joel
she was going to take every precaution she could
to ensure the security of Cassietronics she
thought bitterly. She had learned her lesson well.

'Leave him, Cass,' Peter blurted out, 'leave
him and come to me, you must know how much I
want you.'

Almost Cassie burst into hysterical laughter,
but she stopped herself just in time.

'Peter . . .'

He had crossed the space dividing them and was standing beside her. He glanced downwards and saw the game she was working on.

'A new project?'

Cassie damped down an instinctive reaction to shield her work from his prying eyes.

'Maybe,' she agreed carelessly. 'It's too soon to know yet.'

Once again, Peter's face darkened. 'So not only does he get my intended wife, he gets success handed to him on a plate as well,' he said thickly. 'Well he damn well owes me this . . .'

Before Cassie could stop him he had gripped her arms, jerking her against his body and holding her there with a force she hadn't thought he could exhibit.

Panic flared inside her and she arched back, but instead of deterring him, her panic seemed to have the opposite effect. 'So there is fire beneath all that ice,' he breathed against her skin, his mouth unpleasantly moist as it plundered the arch of her throat.

As she tried to get away from him she felt the belt of her robe slip. As she reached automatically to secure it Peter slid hard fingers into her hair, his eyes caught by the gaping lapel of her robe.

Another moment and he would be touching her breast, Cassie thought sickly, and that was something she could not endure. She would have had to endure it if they had married, she reminded herself, wondering how it was she had lived so many years and known so little about herself. Before meeting Joel Howard she would have described herself as sexually cold, but now . . . She shuddered deeply, almost gagging as she felt Peter's breath fan her lips. She was too frozen to resist him, her brain and body locked and incapable of responding to her instinctive demand for escape.

'Cassie . . .'

'What the hell's going on here?'

Peter released her the instant he heard Joel's voice, turning to face the other man.

Cassie's hand went to the lapel of her robe. She was shivering now with a mixture of fear and relief. Joel looked furiously angry, his navy-blue eyes scorching her with singeing contempt. He could not surely believe she had actively participated in Peter's lovemaking, but apparently he did.

Peter obviously thought so to, because he drawled tauntingly, 'I should have thought it was obvious, Howard. After all Cassie might be your wife, but she and I were engaged . . .' He turned to smile at Cassie. 'I thought you said he wasn't due back, darling,' he murmured, stunning her with his capacity for deceit. 'Pity, I was just beginning to enjoy myself.'

'Out,' Joel grated. 'Now, before I forget I'm supposed to be civilised and break your neck.'

Cassie wasn't surprised when Peter headed for the door. Joel stood to one side as he walked through it. In total silence Cassie heard the front door slam, the silence thickening and stretching until her nerves were coiled like fine wires as Peter started his car and then drove away.

'A very chivalrous lover, you have,' Joel sneered when Peter had gone, 'leaving you to face the wrath of your husband alone . . . What were you doing down here?' he added. 'Weren't the bedrooms good enough for you?'

'Peter had only just arrived,' Cassie told him automatically, not realising how betraying the words sounded until Joel walked towards her. Even without her glasses she was aware of the taut ferocity of his movements. She wanted to turn and run but pride would not let her.

'So you are capable of looking like a woman after all,' Joel said softly as he reached her. He stretched out and brushed his fingers through her hair and Cassie felt her scalp prickle in response. 'And of behaving like one? Perhaps it's time I found out.'

Cassie's automatic denial was lost beneath the angry pressure of his mouth; branding her as though she were his possession she thought numbly as his fingers dug into her arms. His kiss was brutal, almost painfully so and yet some part of her reacted fiercely to the bruising pressure, a well of wild responsiveness rushing up inside her. Her lips parted instinctively, her eyelids heavy with arousal as she tried to focus on the dark blur of Joel's face.

'Damn you,' he muttered thickly releasing her mouth. 'Damn you a thousand times over, but I won't let another man take what is mine.'

His hands left her arms, his fingers tugging at the slack knot of her robe. When she realised what he was doing Cassie gasped in dismayed protest. She must explain to him that he was wrong; that she had not wanted Peter's embraces. His possessive attitude towards her stunned her; it was something she had not expected and she didn't know how to react to it. Her own emotions were too rawly vulnerable for her to be logical.

Her mouth felt soft and bruised from his kiss, the taste of him still lingering on her lips. She licked them tentatively one hand against his chest as she tried to push him away. Beneath his shirt she could feel the heat coming off his skin, and tiny tremors of responsiveness shivered through her.

'What are you doing?' Joel grated. He had untied the knot of her belt, and was tugging it away. Panic spiralled through Cassie, and yet it was a panic spiced with a delirious, blood-heating excitement. 'Comparing his taste to mine?'

The accusation shivered across her nerves. Joel's hands were on the lapels of her robe parting it, sliding over her body, cupping her breasts. 'Does he make you feel like this?'

This time his mouth played with hers, teasing and tormenting her lips into quivering responsiveness until they clung to his and parted eagerly to the conquering thrust of his tongue. Cassie had never been kissed so intimately before, her skin burned, every nerve ending tormented by the onslaught of physical arousal Joel was subjecting her to. As though he knew what was happening to her he made a small male sound of satisfaction into her mouth, his thumbs caressing the already hard tips of her breasts. Cassie felt a wave of shame for their eager responsiveness. Her body seemed to burn with the bitter amalgamation of humiliation and desire—mind warred with body—her senses were winning out, she thought weakly, as wave after wave of bitter-sweet pleasure swept over her. When Joel touched her she became mindless, a puppet capable only of responding to his commands.

He released her mouth and she sighed her

relief, feeling sanity slip back once she was no longer subjected to his physical domination. His hands still cupped her breasts, but she tried to pull away, believing that he had finished punishing her.

He refused to let her go, his hands sliding round her back, imprisoning her. As she arched away from him he lowered his head, his mouth exploring the exposed arch of her throat.

Weakness robbed her of the ability to resist. Her senses were so highly attuned to him that she could barely endure the mingling of pleasure and anguish his touch evoked. His mouth explored her skin with leisurely relaxation, almost as though he knew of her humiliating inability to pull away from him. Sensation after sensation swamped her, shocking her with their intensity. She wanted to reach out and touch him in response, to run her fingertips over the hard muscles of his chest and back, to touch her lips to his skin, to . . . Shivers convulsed her body as she tried to come to terms with the emotions rioting through her. Joel's tongue stroked over the hollow at the base of her neck, slightly rough and infinitely arousing. His mouth moved downward, and she tensed, arching frantically away, self preservation urging her to resist, to fight against the hold he had on her senses while she still could, but his hand against the small of her back, imprisoned the lower half of her body against his while the other curved round her breast.

The downward descent of his mouth towards her breast was something Cassie could not prevent. The light pressure of his mouth against her skin seemed to burn and torment, as though he knew how torn she was between escaping from him and giving in to her need to clasp his head against her body. Deep shudders tore through her. This could not be happening to her; it was beyond the power of any man to reduce her to the mind jellying state of physical arousal. That's all it was, she told herself frantically, physical arousal, and she ought to have the self control to be able to resist it. She hadn't felt a thing other than revulsion when Peter touched her, a small treacherous inner voice reminded her. That reminder only served to increase her terror, but even as she fought against her desire Joel's tongue was drawing erotic circles round her nipple, sending her whirling crazily out of control to a place where the whole universe centred round the pleasure-inducing brush of his tongue and the eager, urgent ache in her breasts, and she yearned wantonly against her will for his more intimate possession.

When his tongue finally brushed over the throbbing apex of her breast Cassie abandoned all her attempts to resist her emotions. Her hands left his chest where they had been braced to resist him, clinging instead to the breadth of his shoulders, her head tipped back, her breath coming in long, shuddering sobs.

'My God, no wonder he wanted you.'

She heard Joel mutter the words, but could make no sense of them. He added something she couldn't catch, and groaned huskily, a deep shudder tensing his body against hers, as his mouth opened over her breast.

His teeth grated slightly over her responsive flesh and she moaned softly, arching frantically against him, deaf to everything but the tormenting moan of need building up inside her. She cried out aloud as Joel sucked compulsively on her breast, pierced by sensations so unfamiliar that they half frightened her. Her body seemed to be possessed by alien emotions so strong that it was impossible to deny them.

'I want you.' Joel's hands moved down over her body, holding her hips, his mouth seeking her other breast. His skin burned beneath his shirt; he was breathing heavily, his hands trembling faintly as he caressed her in rapidly urgent strokes.

He was aroused and he wanted her Cassie realised, and suddenly the realisation hit her that that was all there was to it. He wanted her to satisfy an entirely masculine and physical appetite, while she ... her mind shied away from the thoughts filling it. She what, she asked herself tensely. She loved him? How could she? She barely knew him. And yet the tiny thought once formed would not be denied. She stiffened in Joel's arms, catching him off-guard enough to step away from him. He studied her, his eyes dark and blank, a dull flush heating his skin.

'We can't,' Cassie told him shakily, pulling her robe protectively round herself.

'Why not? We're married—remember?' He was still caught up in his sexual need for her, Cassie realised, and yet she could not allow him to make love to her simply to satisfy that need. He didn't want her as a person.

How could she stop him? Her mind sought for an answer, and found one. Forcing herself to appear calm, she said coolly, 'I'm not on the pill, or anything . . . we could have a child . . .'

'You didn't seem to be too worried about that half an hour ago when I found you with Williams,' Joel retorted harshly.

What could she say to him? That she had been in no danger of succumbing to Peter? What conclusions might he not draw from that revealing comment. She had no illusions left now. If he guessed how emotionally vulnerable she was to him, might he not use that vulnerability to take her company away from her?

Summoning all her courage Cassie faced him squarely and lied, 'If Peter had made me pregnant, it wouldn't matter—after all once I'm free of this marriage to you, Peter and I . . .'

'My God, you're all the same aren't you?' he exploded furiously, not letting her finish. 'Too bad you didn't think it through a little more though, Cassie. I'm far, far richer than Peter Williams will ever be. Just think if I'd fathered a child on you, you might have been able to force me into continuing our marriage.'

Taking a deep breath Cassie flung bitterly at him, 'Money might be everything to you, Joel, but it isn't to me, and besides you're forgetting I have enough and earn enough to provide for any child I might ultimately have, on my own. I would never pressure any man into supporting me because I'd had his child, and I would never contemplate having a child by any man I did not respect and . . .'

'All right,' he cut in harshly. 'You've made your point. I'm the last man on earth you'd want as the father of your child, but just remember,

Cassie, while you're married to me, you'll behave accordingly. If I think you're playing around with Williams behind my back, I'll make you both sorry you were ever born. If he becomes your lover . . .'

'What makes you think he isn't already?' Cassie challenged, bitter that he should assume she was so undesirable that no man had ever been her lover, even though it was true. He had mocked her for her virginity before, and suddenly it angered her.

'There's one sure way to find out,' he said softly, coming towards her and gripping her chin with firm fingers. 'Is that what you want me to do, Cassie? Make love to you?'

'No.' She jerked away from him, turning her face away so that he wouldn't see the betraying sweep of hot colour his words aroused.

'Then you haven't been lovers?' he persisted.

What should she say? That until he realised that Joel had married her, Peter had never even contemplated making love to her? No, that would be too humiliating.

'Not yet,' she agreed as casually as she could. As she turned to face him she thought for a moment she saw a gleam of satisfaction darken his eyes, but her eyesight was so poor without her glasses she felt sure she must have imagined it.

'Not yet and not ever, as long as you remain married to me,' he warned her softly, 'just remember that, Cassie.'

He didn't say what retaliatory measure he would take if she didn't but Cassie thought shiveringly that she had no desire to find out.

'I've brought down your computer,' he told

her, completely changing the subject. 'I'll install it in here for you.' He glanced at the papers she had been working on, and frowned. 'A new game?'

'Maybe,' Cassie agreed non-committally.

Suddenly his eyes narrowed, 'I hope you aren't thinking of revenging yourself on me by giving a new game to Williams, Cassie?'

Her mouth tightened. Did he always have to think the very worst of people?

'I hadn't thought of giving it to anyone. At the moment it's just a series of ideas,' she told him curtly.

'But you were entertaining Williams here in my house, wearing only a bathrobe,' he pointed out tauntingly.

'I'm wearing a bathrobe because having a bath was the only way I could get warm,' Cassie told him bitingly. 'Peter called unexpectedly, in fact when I heard the car I thought . . .' She broke off biting her lip as she recalled how eagerly she had rushed downstairs, believing it was him.

'Yes,' Joel probed softly. 'You thought . . .'

'I thought whoever it was might think the house was empty and go away again,' Cassie lied valiantly, refusing to look at him.

'Umm . . . Well, standing around dressed like that isn't going to make you feel any warmer. You go and get dressed, I'll get the heating on.

As she walked to the door, he added tauntingly, 'Not that I perceived any coldness about you, Cassie. As a matter of fact . . .'

She slammed the door on him before he could finish his goading statement, rich colour stealing up under her skin. She hated him she thought crossly, really really hated him.

During the next few days Cassie found herself examining that statement as she watched Joel installing her computer, interspersing it with doing some of his own work, and was forced to acknowledge that far from hating him she was dangerously close to loving him. Too close to draw back. Just having him in the house with her brought her a happiness that made her shiver with fear for her future. How had it happened? She barely knew him. Some things defied logic she was forced to admit, and her love for Joel Howard was obviously one of them. All she could do now was pray that he never discovered it.

CHAPTER SIX

A WEEK slipped by and Joel continued to stay at Howard Court. Cassie devised elaborate methods of avoiding him without being seen to do so. The fact that he had a considerable amount of work to do made this easier. After breakfast each morning he shut himself away in his study, very rarely emerging before mid-afternoon.

When he was busy he didn't bother with lunch, he told Cassie when she asked what he wanted her to do about meals.

With Mary Jensen's aid she had organised a firm to come and clean both the carpets and the upholstery in the downstairs rooms. A Mrs Pollit from the village had agreed to come and clean three mornings a week. At first Cassie was slightly apprehensive that Joel might consider she had taken too much upon herself in view of her very temporary status as his wife, but to her surprise he said nothing, merely frowning slightly when he strode into the drawing room and found the furniture shrouded in covers.

'I've arranged for the painters to come and touch up the paintwork,' she told him hesitantly. 'This is such a beautiful room it seems a shame to let it get neglected, but if you'd rather I didn't . . .'

'Do whatever you like,' he told her brusquely, glancing frowningly round the room. 'In fact change the entire colour scheme if you feel like it.'

Cassie sensed that he almost hoped she would. Anything rather than live with the legacy of his mother's presence she thought wryly, but the former Mrs Howard had had excellent taste, and Cassie had fallen in love on sight with the mellow golds and soft blues of the drawing room.

Mrs Pollit had just left for the day when Joel walked into the kitchen and announced that he had to drive up to London.

'I need some papers from my office,' he explained curtly, frowning as he looked at her. 'You look pale,' he told her shortly. 'What's the matter—missing Williams' attentions? Well don't look to me to supply them in lieu.'

It seemed that he could barely speak to her without insulting her Cassie thought miserably when he had gone. There was an angry tension about him recently that made her heart contract with pain every time he looked at her.

That he deeply resented her presence in his life she couldn't doubt, and yet she couldn't find the willpower to remind him that his burden was self-inflicted.

Fortunately her own business could be run with the aid of a telephone and from her desk in the library. Her secretary was handling the day to day mundane chores, and Joel had made arrangements for all her mail to be forwarded on to her. With Joel gone she went into the library, and got out her notes on her new game. She never worked on it while he was around, terrified that his astute mind would all too easily make the connection between the design of the new game and her feelings for him. It would be her farewell gift to him she thought achingly, the price of her freedom from a marriage that was becoming daily more onerous—not because it existed, but because of the form in which it existed. It was like being allowed the merest glimpse of paradise and then told one could never hope to look at it again, she reflected, frowning as she considered the viability of working such an idea into her game—it could be the ultimate goal of the player. She laughed a little bitterly. Why on earth had she been stupid enough to fall in love with Joel? At least before she met him she had been content with her life; clear-headed enough to know her limitations and to live by them. Since he had erupted into her tightly enclosed world she had been subject to an entire range of unattainable dreams, chief of which was lying in Joel's arms while he told her he loved her.

It was hopeless, she decided, annoyed with herself, now she couldn't even shut Joel out while she worked. A cup of coffee might help her to think more objectively.

She was just leaving the room when the 'phone rang. She reached for the receiver automatically, freezing as she heard a caressingly female voice enquiring, 'Is Joel there?'

There was no reason at all for her to feel the prickle of awareness that shivered down her spine—Joel received many telephone calls during the day from his office and his business associates but intuition told Cassie that this woman was not one of them.

'I'm afraid he isn't,' she replied as calmly as she could. 'Would you like to leave a message?'

'No it doesn't matter,' the voice responded carelessly, 'I'll be seeing him later. 'Bye . . .'

So Joel wasn't just going to London on business, she thought painfully. Was that the reason for his growing tension? A sexual frustration that could find no outlet while he remained with her? The thought was gallingly painful, and Cassie tried to shut it out as she walked numbly into the kitchen, just as she tried to shut out the tormenting images filling her mind of Joel making love to some other woman. The images were far too vivid; far too erotic. Her hands shook as she reached for a cup. It shattered on the floor as it slipped from her fingers and suddenly Cassie found that she was crying, tearing abandoned sobs of pain torturing her throat, making her whole body ache with an anguish for which there was no panacea.

She didn't hear the kitchen door open, freezing in shock as she felt the hand on her shoulder.

The woman looking at her with sympathy and compassion was unknown to her, and yet at the same time instantly recognisable. Joel had inherited his mother's eyes Cassie thought bemusedly, and it was also from her that he got his dark hair. Hers was faintly streaked with grey, caught back in a smooth chignon that revealed the delicate purity of a bone structure that would make her a beautiful woman even in old age.

Slim and elegantly dressed in vivid silk separates, she presented the sort of image Cassie normally shrank away from, knowing how she herself must look in comparison, but those navy-blue eyes, so like her son's and yet so warm and understanding, melted the barriers of her reserve.

Almost without being aware of it Cassie allowed herself to be led to a chair and pushed gently into it. Seconds, or was it minutes later, she was sipping gratefully from a mug of fragrant coffee, the kitchen restored to pristine order.

'So, you're Joel's wife, and these . . .' graceful fingers touched the dampness of Cassie's cheek gently, 'are no doubt occasioned by my obtuse and obstinate son.'

'How did you know?' Cassie asked bemusedly, ignoring the last part of the question. 'How did you know who I was?'

'I recognised you from a photograph of you I saw in a paper.' A trace of sadness touched her mouth. 'It's just as well I always take the English papers, otherwise I'd never have known that Joel had married. But then no doubt he considers that I don't deserve to know. My son takes a great delight in punishing others for what he considers their sins, but then I suspect you've discovered this for yourself?'

'Mary Jensen told me about you,' Cassie responded awkwardly, 'about what happened.'

'And you discovered for yourself how my son chooses to regard me?'

Cassie looked away. It was plain that his mother thought the world of Joel, and it was equally plain that she knew exactly how he felt about her.

'I was very surprised to read that Joel had married.'

Cassie flushed, knowing that his mother must be thinking, especially to such a plain creature, and suddenly the need to tell someone the truth became unbearable.

'Only because he needs my company,' she began bitterly, and then soon it was all pouring out, not just her marriage to Joel, but things she had never dreamed of telling anyone, fears that had tormented her for years; the pain of being plain and unloved, the agonies she had endured as a teenager.

When it was over Miranda said quietly, 'You love him don't you?'

For a moment Cassie was too stunned to reply and then she said unevenly, 'Am I so obvious?'

A reassuring smile restored some of her equilibrium. 'Only to someone who's suffered the same thing. I think you have good grounds for hating me Cassie. To a large extent it's my fault that Joel is the way he is.' Sadness darkened her eyes. 'I tried so hard to do what was best, but ... I have a plan,' she said suddenly, a smile breaking through. 'I've always wanted a daughter, Cassie, and it would please me very much if you would accept me as a sort of honorary godmother for a while.'

She radiated warmth and love Cassie thought, blinking a little. She could rarely remember ever being so drawn to anyone before, and it saddened her to think that Joel had deliberately denied himself the pleasure of having such a person in his life. Whatever the rights and wrongs of what she had done Miranda was a woman who could only enrich the lives of everyone she met.

'Come on, go upstairs and wash your face. I'll make us both an omelette and then when we've eaten it we'll sit down and talk. When do you expect my errant son back, by the way?'

Cassie bit her lip and then said in a low voice.

'I'm not sure. There was a telephone call for him a while ago. A ... woman. It may be that he won't be back until tomorrow.'

'Oh.'

The small word held so much; understanding, kindness, compassion, and Cassie pushed back her chair, wanting to escape from the room before she broke down again.

When she got back downstairs true to her word Miranda had prepared for them a deliciously fluffy omelette but Cassie could not do it justice.

Miranda was a warmly entertaining companion, and in other circumstances Cassie knew she would have been more amused by her anecdotes about her life in Florence.

'You seem very happy,' she said wistfully at one point, observing the tender expression in Miranda's eyes as she talked about her second husband.

'More so perhaps than I deserve,' Miranda agreed quietly, 'although I can never forget that my happiness was bought by the death of one of my sons and the loss of the other.'

'Oh no ...' impulsively Cassie reached out towards her. 'Andrew's death was a tragedy, but not your fault.'

'Not morally perhaps, but emotionally ... ah that is another matter. Joel was always my favourite,' she added, confirming what Mary Jensen had already said, and when Cassie told her this, her face lit up. 'Mary is still living here? I must try and see her, she was always such a good friend and wise counsellor to me.'

'Joel believes you preferred Andrew to him,' Cassie told her. 'I'm afraid ...'

'That he is a bitter, resentful man who stubbornly clings to the prejudices of his childhood, refusing to re-assess them through the eyes of an adult? Yes, I know,' she agreed sadly. 'I have come to believe that Joel has more of his father in him than I once thought, and it seems to me that you are paying the price for what he sees as my sins.'

'I sometimes suspect he despises the entire female race,' Cassie sighed. 'Oh, he has scores of beautiful women-friends, but deep down inside I don't believe he genuinely cares about any of them.' She saw the expression on her companion's face and gave her a painful smile, 'Oh don't worry, I'm not suffering from any illusions, if Joel was asked to make a choice I know he'd choose a beautiful rather than a plain woman every time.'

'You consider yourself plain? My dear you are not,' Miranda told her, 'merely in need of a little gilding.'

'You forget, it is only elegant flowers like lilies that benefit from gilding, common or garden daisies it merely highlights their ordinariness.'

'Nonsense,' Miranda told her crisply, suddenly very like her autocratic son. 'You have far too low an opinion of yourself Cassie, something which I'm sure my charming son has been at pains to foster. Tell me, when Joel snatched you away so impulsively was there no young man at hand to take umbrage at his high-handed behaviour.?'

'Only Peter Williams,' Cassie told her, adding, 'I told you, we were engaged . . .'

'Yes, of course . . . I take it you have seen nothing of him since?'

'Well no, he did come here to see me.' Briefly Cassie explained what had happened, just managing to conceal the rich tide of colour threatening to swamp her pale skin as she remembered how Joel had reacted to Peter's visit, but that was hardly something she could discuss with his mother.

'Umm . . .' The dark blue eyes looked at her shrewdly, but Miranda added nothing to her original comment.

At ten o'clock by mutual consent they both went to bed. Miranda had had a tiring day, having flown from Italy that morning and come straight from Heathrow in a hired car. She could not stay long, she told Cassie, but she wanted to stay long enough to see her son.

They were halfway through the next day before she got her wish. Cassie was chatting to Miranda as they drank coffee in the library when she heard a car outside. Seconds later she heard Joel's firm tread across the hall. As he reached the library door he called out sharply, 'Cassie, that car outside, who does it belong to?'

Cassie was saved the need of responding as Miranda walked calmly towards the door. Framed within its aperture she said softly, 'It's mine, Joel.'

Cassie had thought she had seen him looking bitter and angry before, but it had been nothing compared with his present expression.

'What the hell are you doing here?' he demanded harshly, striding towards the door.

'I came to introduce myself to your wife, seeing as you seem disinclined to do so,' Miranda responded mildly, not seeming at all concerned by his fury, while Cassie flinched back, nervously aware of the tense undercurrents infiltrating the room.

'Well now that you've introduced yourself, you can leave,' Joel announced tersely after a few seconds' silence. 'I told you once before, I won't have you here . . .'

His harsh cruelty provoked Cassie into a shocked protest. 'Joel, she's your mother,' she told him, for once oblivious to the warning signs darkening the irises of his eyes.

'Oh yes, she's my mother, and because she *is* my mother, I'm left to guess at the identity of my father. Something she probably doesn't even know herself.'

The bitterness of his words; the total un-expectedness of them stunned both women for a second. Miranda was the first to recover, her voice only slightly tremulous as she said quietly, 'You are being both insulting and unfair, Joel. Whatever my other sins, I can assure you that I never had a child by anyone other than my first husband . . .'

Navy-blue eyes held navy-blue, while on the sidelines Cassie held her breath. A little to her surprise Joel was the first to look away. 'I want you to leave,' he said tersely, but some of the intense bitterness seemed to have left his voice.

'So I shall, once Cassie has packed her things,' Miranda agreed lightly, smiling sunnily as though unaware of the effect of her words on the pair studying her.

'Packed her . . .' Abruptly Joel switched his attention from his mother to Cassie. 'What the hell . . .'

'Cassie is coming back to Florence with me for a little holiday. The poor child looks exhausted, Joel, and besides I want a chance to get to know my new daughter-in-law.'

'Cassie tell her you're not going,' Joel demanded ominously.

On the point of doing so, Cassie remembered that he had come to her after spending the evening and perhaps even the night with another woman; that he had treated her with thinly disguised contempt from the start; and that if she stayed she was running the danger of him discovering her shaming secret. Without giving herself time to think she took a deep breath.

'I am going Joel,' she told him firmly.

'I see.' His lips thinned angrily as he studied her with cold eyes. 'And when may I expect you back?'

'You will get her back my son, when you come to collect her,' Miranda answered for her.

For a handful of seconds Joel glared at them both, and then turning abruptly on his heel he stormed out of the house. Cassie waited until the sound of his car engine had died away before saying slowly, 'Did you mean that Miranda, about taking me back to Florence with you?'

'Every word of it,' Miranda assured her softly. 'It came to me last night that it would be just the thing. I told you I wanted to play godmother, Cassie. Joel prefers beautiful women you told me, well between us we're going to turn you into a woman so beautiful that my obnoxious son will be dumbfounded.'

'Impossible,' Cassie told her quietly, 'I know you mean well Miranda, but I faced the truth about myself years ago. I'm plain.'

'You *think* you're plain,' Miranda corrected her, 'and you've told yourself that you are for so long that you behave as though you are; and even worse, you encourage other people to adopt the same attitude to you. Where's your spirit Cassie? Don't you want to give Joel a taste of his own medicine?'

Doubtfully Cassie stared at her. Was Miranda just using her to get at Joel. One glance into the warm, kind face of the other woman assured her. No, Miranda wasn't like that.

'Trust me, Cassie,' she said softly, 'and have faith, both in yourself and me. Tell yourself that you are beautiful, and I promise you you will be. Real beauty comes from the inside anyway, as all women know, but men being the weak creatures that they are are always dazzled by outward allure rather than inner beauty, you already have the latter, and it will be my task, and my pleasure to give you the former.'

'Nico, look who I have brought back with me.'

They were through Italian customs and being escorted to a waiting car by a tall, distinguished-looking Italian, who at first had made Cassie feel a little nervous. It was all very well for Miranda to say that her husband would be delighted to see her, but Cassie was wondering if that were true?

One look from the smiling dark brown eyes turned in her direction assured her. They twinkled warmly; their warmth spiced by appreciative male interest.

'So this is Joel's bride? He has at last forgiven you then has he *cara*, that he allows you to bring her back with you?'

'I'm afraid not.' As Miranda made the admission Cassie was aware of the deep bond of sympathy flowing from Nico to his wife. 'If anything Joel has become even more firmly entrenched in his own hostile world. I have Cassie's permission to tell you about their marriage, which I shall do just as soon as we have had something to eat.'

This was something she and Cassie had discussed on the 'plane and Cassie had willingly given her agreement to her suggestion that she told Nico the true circumstances of their marriage.

'Cassie, ably assisted by my son, has succeeded in persuading herself that she is a dull pebble of no account, while I perceive within her a diamond only in need of some skilled polishing.'

Cassie flushed a little under Nico's kind scrutiny, wondering if he actually believed what his wife was saying, or if he merely thought she was being kind, as Cassie did herself. But what if Miranda was right ... what if ... but no, it was pointless to speculate, to imagine Joel looking at her with anything than other cold disdain. Hadn't she always despised women who valued themselves purely on their looks and yet here she was longing to believe that Miranda was right when she said she could be beautiful.

Sighing faintly Cassie directed her attention away from herself and towards her surroundings. Florence was a beautiful city, basking now in the late May sunshine.

The Fontinis owned a villa outside the town, surrounded by pleasant secluded gardens. The villa was old and elegant, the furniture in the large reception hallway obviously antique.

'You look tired,' Miranda sympathised as she looked at Cassie's wan face. 'I telephoned Maria to prepare a room for you. I'll show you up to it, so that you can rest. Tomorrow we start to go to work on polishing the diamond Cassie, so make sure you get plenty of rest this afternoon.'

Behind them Nico laughed. 'Ah I must warn you Cassie that my wife is indefatigable when she sets her mind to a particular course.'

They were still deeply in love, anyone could see that, and yet Cassie knew instinctively that for Miranda her happiness was overshadowed by Andrew's death and Joel's hostility.

The room Miranda showed her to was large, with a high ceiling, and beautiful carved antique furniture. A large rug in soft pinks and greens covered the floor, the curtains and bedspread picking out the same faded pink.

There was a bathroom off the bedroom with marble fitments and walls. More grand than Howard Court, the villa still had an air of being lived in and loved.

Nico, Cassie had learned owned and ran a factory producing tractors and other farming equipment. 'Once his family considered themselves too noble to concern themselves with trade, but now if it weren't for the profits from the factory, the villa and its contents would have to be sold. Nico has a son from his first marriage. You will like Bernardo. At present he is away on business, but he will return at the end of the week.'

Cassie hadn't realised that Miranda had a stepson; and indeed that Nico possessed a large family of sisters and cousins, all of whom would be very eager to meet her, Miranda assured her. 'Don't look so worried,' she laughed when she saw the frown pucker Cassie's face. 'I will not allow them to eat you and you will see none of them until we have worked a little magic.'

Quite what magic Miranda had in mind Cassie did not know, but strangely as she did her bidding and lay down on her vast bed for a rest she found herself quite content to leave everything in Miranda's hands. It must be the Italian air, she decided drowsily because suddenly all things seemed possible, even her own transformation.

Her last thoughts before sleep claimed her were of Joel. What was he doing now? Had he gone back to London; to the woman with the sultry voice? Curling herself into a tight ball, Cassie refused to make herself miserable thinking about him. 'I am beautiful,' she muttered fiercely to herself as her eyes closed. 'I am beautiful ... I am ...'

CHAPTER SEVEN

'FIRST things first,' Miranda announced over breakfast the following morning. Nico had already left for his office and so the two women had the breakfast room to themselves. 'A woman who considers herself beautiful moves with a certain confidence; not arrogance, but a confirmation of her own self-worth. I have enrolled you, Cassie, at a small private school in Florence, where the daughters of families such as Nico's spend a few weeks after leaving school.'

'A sort of finishing course?' Cassie murmured, visions of herself being forced to endure the curious looks of a roomful of pretty teenagers making her shrink almost physically.

'A cross between that and what in Britain would be called a "grooming course",' Miranda agreed, 'but you need have no fears or qualms, I have arranged for you to have your tuition privately. Madame Bonare will come here to the villa each morning to teach you. In her day she was a famous ballerina, and even at seventy years of age, she is still one of the most elegant women I have ever seen. She will teach you to see your body as it really is, to assess its potential and its drawbacks, and how to promote the former above the latter.'

Cassie felt quite overwhelmed.

'It is fortunate that you are so slender,' Miranda commented, 'that gives you an im-

mediate advantage when it comes to wearing
clothes.' She grimaced faintly as she studied the
fawn skirt and blouse Cassie was wearing. 'At the
moment you look as though you wish to fade into
the wallpaper. Beige is not a colour you should
wear with your skin Cassie ... and we must do
something about your hair ... I will speak to
Carlo ... Oh I am going to enjoy having you
staying here,' she added smiling at Cassie.

Madame Bonare arrived an hour later. Feeling
very self-conscious in the leotard Miranda had
lent her, Cassie smiled hesitantly as the introductions were performed. Once she had exchanged
pleasantries with her guest Miranda left Cassie
alone with her in the half-empty long gallery that
ran the length of the villa.

'So ...' Madame murmured, studying Cassie
closely, 'Miranda is right. Everything is there,
but you are not making the most of it are you?'

To receive such a pronouncement startled
Cassie who had been expecting the elegant,
almost formidable older woman to declare that
there was simply nothing she could do with such
poor raw material.

'You must not slouch so ...' she told Cassie,
placing her hands on Cassie's shoulders and
forcing them back. 'You have good bones,' she
continued, 'both in the face and in the body. You
are slim, which is good, but you do not carry
yourself well. And why do you hunch your chest
so?'

Unhappily Cassie explained her dislike of her
to her own mind too generously rounded breasts.

'If you were wishing to be a fashion model I

would agree with you,' Madame told her, 'but for a woman a pretty bosom is always an asset.'

Her use of the old-fashioned word made Cassie smile a little, and her teacher made good use of her relaxation to get her to walk up and down the room.

'When you walk you look at the floor, do not. Walk as though you are proud of yourself. Carry your body proudly, always, always remember that.'

Two hours later feeling absolutely exhausted Cassie bid her teacher goodbye. She had just emerged from her bathroom when Miranda knocked and then walked excitedly into her bedroom.

'Nina is very pleased with you,' she told a surprised Cassie. 'She says you have the elegance for which Englishwomen are known.'

'She said I have good bones,' Cassie told her, still half amazed herself by this announcement.

'So you have,' Miranda agreed. 'I have spoken to Carlo and this afternoon we are to go and see him. Then afterwards we shall visit my beauty salon.' When she saw Cassie's expression she smiled at her. 'Beauty, like any other asset has to be polished my love, but it will all be worthwhile, you will see.'

And see she did, Cassie reflected nearly a week later, as she surveyed her reflection in her bedroom mirror. She had just spent an arduous two hours with Madame, exercising, and her skin glowed a softly pretty peach, her hair, cut and layered into a flattering style that encouraged it to wave softly round her face, shining softly where the sunlight touched it.

Yesterday she had had her first make-up lesson and had been astounded by the difference properly applied cosmetics made to her face. Bemused she had stared at her own reflection in the beauty salon mirror, wondering if this elegant creature with the high cheek bones and huge, hazel-green eyes really was Cassie Howard.

And to prevent her from hiding her newly sculptured beauty behind a barrier of plastic and glass, Miranda discovered and exploited Cassie's long-suppressed desire to be rid of her glasses. After hours of tests in a Florentine opticians, she had emerged with rapidly blinking, unbespectacled eyes—rejoicing in her new soft contact lenses—to see the city and herself with greater clarity.

Highlights subtly applied to her newly cut hair gave it a rich chestnut glow that the Italian sunshine would enhance, Carlo had assured her. The hair she had considered so thin and poor seemed suddenly under Carlo's clever fingers to have changed into a glorious thick mane of tawny richness, its shape emphasising the subtle contours of her face.

Daily exercise had brought a glow to her skin and a new assurance to her movements; she was blossoming, Cassie recognised, perhaps rather a late bloomer, but blooming in a way she had never envisaged possible for her, and it was all thanks to Miranda.

Whenever she had despaired or felt awkward Joel's mother had been there to encourage and commiserate. When Madame called her clumsy and gauche, as she goaded her on, Miranda always seemed to sense her despair and have a few words of praise to restore her self-confidence.

'Excellent,' Madame had pronounced during this morning's lesson, as Cassie walked the length of the room for her. 'Excellent—now at last you are saying to the world, "I am a woman of great worth and charm—look at me and perceive that for yourself"—and believe me that is exactly what the world will do *cara*—it will value as highly or as unworthily as you value yourself. Tell it you are well pleased with yourself and it will support your judgment—tell it you are not; that you find yourself unworthy and unworthwhile and it too will judge you thus.'

'Cassie?'

'Coming,' Cassie called out, recognising Miranda's voice outside her door. This afternoon they were going out window shopping. As yet Cassie was to buy nothing Miranda had told her. For the present they would simply study style and colour.

'A woman who is truly secure in herself knows instinctively what suits her and wears it regardless of fashion's dictates.'

Thanks to her visits to Miranda's beauty therapist Cassie's skin no longer looked muddy and dull, but gleamed with health and care, her manner vital and outward looking where it had been withdrawn and dull. She found she was actually looking forward to going out; that she no longer dreaded being the object of people's curiosity.

Pulling a brush through her hair, she give her reflection a final glance.

'Very good,' Miranda approved, scrutinising her make-up when she opened the door. 'You are a quick study *cara*, and you look very lovely.'

As always Miranda's praise warmed her. Cassie had not heard a single word from Joel since she left home. Had he forgotten completely that he had a wife she wondered achingly. Would he come and get her as Miranda had decreed? Somehow she thought not.

Seven days turned into ten and then fourteen, and Cassie no longer found it strange to catch a glimpse of herself in a mirror or shop window and wonder at the identity of the slender smiling girl with the cloud of rich dark hair and pale creamy skin who she saw there.

With Miranda's gentle guidance she had re-stocked her wardrobe with rich blues and soft yellows in supple silk, and pastel cottons. Not one item of the new clothes she had bought was beige, or anything approaching that colour. Each day added a little to her growing confidence, and Cassie found that the boost to her self confidence of knowing she looked good made her much warmer and more open in her approach to other people. Shop assistants whom she would once have shrunk away from now smiled welcomingly at her, and she had gained enough confidence to make a few shopping forays on her own, practising her growing skill with Italian.

She had been in Florence nearly three weeks when Miranda mentioned Joel for the first time.

'Have you heard anything from him?' she enquired as they shared their breakfast table.

Cassie shook her head. Joel's angry silence was something she had come to live with. Along with her increased self confidence had come the realisation that even transformed as she was Joel was hardly likely to fall at her feet. And did she really want him to? She loved him she knew that, but what she wanted in return was his love of her as a person, not an image.

'Don't worry, you will,' Miranda reassured her, adding perceptively, 'If you still want to?'

'I still love him,' Cassie admitted, 'But . . .'

'I know.' Miranda touched her fingers lightly. 'Cassie I've enjoyed having you here so much and I hope that whatever happens between you and Joel, you will always consider me at least as a friend . . .'

'As my fairy godmother,' Cassie assured her. It was true. No matter what the future might hold there would always be a special place in her heart for Miranda, and for Nico, who had lavished generous amounts of male appreciation and encouragement on her first stumbling efforts to transform herself, and who now Cassie saw in the light of a particularly well-loved uncle.

'You have blossomed even beyond my imaginings,' Miranda told her, 'and I think to celebrate both your transformation and Nico's birthday we shall have a party.'

Where once she had dreaded such gatherings Cassie now found herself plunging enthusiastically into all the arrangements acting as Miranda's unofficial secretary, and learning as she did how efficient the older woman was.

'We shall both need new dresses,' Miranda proclaimed when they had finished checking the guest list together. 'I have arranged for the gardens to be flood-lit, and I think this is an occasion when we can both give in to the temptation to glow as brightly as any fireflies.

Bernardo will be home in time for the party. I rang him in Brussels yesterday to check.'

'You get on well with him?' Cassie queried, wondering if Nico's son had objected to their marriage as strongly as Joel.

'Extremely well.' Miranda's eyes twinkled, 'Bernardo is a very charming and flirtatious young man I must warn you, Cassie. He is also an extremely susceptible one . . .'

'But not one to be taken seriously,' Cassie guessed laughing.

'You will like him,' Miranda assured her, 'and he will make good target practice, if you wish to perfect your flirting.' She laughed at Cassie's startled expression. 'My dear, every woman must know how to flirt, it is part of the art of being charming, and Bernardo will take no harm from it. In fact it will probably teach him a thing or two.'

They spent the afternoon browsing round the shops, visiting Miranda's favourite boutique in their search for suitable dresses.

Miranda with her dark hair and dark blue eyes looked stunning in Italian silks and Cassie wasn't surprised when she opted for a dress in varying shades of her favourite blue. Both elegant and feminine, Cassie immediately applauded her choice.

'Now we have to find something for you,' Miranda commented when she re-emerged from the changing rooms. 'Something very, very special.'

'The party is for Nico, not me,' Cassie protested, but Miranda's thoughts were obviously elsewhere, a preoccupied look in her eyes.

'I know the very place,' she announced at length, 'Come on.'

She took Cassie not to a shop but to a small salon up a steep flight of stairs in the old part of the town. The small dark haired woman who came to greet them, let loose a burst of fluid Italian too rapid for Cassie to follow.

'Signora Tonli makes the gowns for all our prettiest brides, Cassie,' Miranda explained. 'Come here and let her have a look at you.'

'But I'm not a bride,' Cassie protested, a little unnerved by the small woman's scrutiny.

'In Italy a girl is a bride throughout her first year of marriage *cara*. Joel robbed me of the chance of seeing you dressed as a bride should be on your wedding day, but . . .'

'I don't think I could wear white,' Cassie murmured, not wanting to hurt Miranda's feelings, but uncertain exactly what she had in mind.

Miranda laughed. 'No, I don't intend to go that far . . .' She spoke rapidly to Signora Tonli who quickly produced a pencil and pad, rapidly sketching something on it, in between brief, but assessing glances at Cassie.

'Signora Tonli and I both agree that pale green would be a particularly effective colour for you. It will bring out the sheen of your skin and the green tints of your eyes. Also it is a colour few Italian girls wear because of their darker skin. This is what she has in mind.' Miranda showed Cassie the sketch.

The dress depicted was a Victorian fantasy of puffed sleeves, tiny waist and full, flounced skirt, caught up with tiny bunches of artificial flowers.

'I could never wear anything like that,' Cassie began to demur, but something about the sheer femininity of the sketch held her. It was a romantic daydream of a dress, a once in a lifetime real live ballgown such as she had never ever imagined herself wearing. At one time she would have genuinely believed that for someone to suggest she wore such a dress would have been sheer malicious cruelty. Indecision clouded her eyes.

'Trust me,' Miranda whispered softly, and remembering all her kindnesses and compassion Cassie gave way.

'If you think it will be all right,' she agreed uncertainly.

'All right?' Miranda raised her eyebrows, 'My dear, you will be sensational . . . a fairy princess . . . the belle of the ball, I promise you . . .'

Miranda had arranged to hold the party the Saturday after Nico's birthday, by which time Cassie would have been with them over a month. Not once during that time had she heard from Joel, her only communications from London being the reports and other necessary papers relating to her business that she received from his secretary.

She had worked in a desultory fashion on her new game during her stay in Florence, but there had been so many other things to do, so much to see that she was beginning to feel almost guilty about her laziness.

During the week before the ball Miranda seemed unusually edgy but Cassie put this down to her concern that all should go well. Cassie had

had three fittings for her gown, and Carlo, Miranda's hairdresser had also been given specific instructions by Miranda as to what was required.

'I hope I'm not going to look over-dressed,' Cassie murmured uneasily listening to them. As a hangover from the days when all she had wanted to do was to fade out of sight, she still felt a little worried about attracting undue attention, although the manners of the average Italian male had largely banished that. Cassie had grown used to the smiles and admiring comments she received whenever she went out. She had lost count of the number of attractive young men who had approached her in the street, even when she was out with Miranda. Italy definitely went to a girl's head, she reflected one afternoon from a successful expedition to find Nico a birthday present.

Cassie knew the city quite well by now, and knowing Nico's love of antiques she had searched carefully for exactly the right thing to give him, finding it in a delicately enamelled Sèvres snuff box, whose price made her blink and then reflect how very pleasant it was to be able to repay Nico's hospitality with a present that she knew would genuinely please.

She had never spent so much money in her life as she was doing at present, she thought wryly, hurrying back to where she had left Miranda's small car. But then she had earned it ... and before there had been nothing and no one to spend it on apart from herself. In Miranda and Nico she had found friends whose love and affection sometimes almost reduced her to silly tears. They both cared so genuinely about her; about her as herself, she acknowledged slipping into the small Fiat. Both of them were delighted by her transformation but delighted for her. Miranda as she was fond of pointing out had known from the very first that the raw material was there, and Nico frequently told her that it was a pleasure to see her pretty face across the table, to hear her laughing and to know that in her Miranda had found the daughter she had always wanted.

'Our only regret is that in reality you are not our child,' he had told Cassie simply only the previous evening when she had declined when they invited her to go out to dinner with them, protesting that they must be growing tired of her constant presence in their home.

In fact all that marred her happiness was Joel's continued silence. Would he come for her? Cassie doubted it. Perhaps he was even hoping that she would remain in Italy for the entire remainder of the six months he had stipulated their marriage must last, thus saving himself the chore of having to continue the pretence.

When she said as much to Miranda on the evening of Nico's birthday she frowned and said slowly, 'And if he does not come for you would you stay here *cara*, or would you go back?'

'I think I should stay here,' Cassie responded, half surprising herself with the admission.

'Good,' Miranda praised her softly. 'My son doesn't know what he is missing—in more ways than one. You have all the virtues any mother could want in a daughter-in-law Cassie. Loyalty, intelligence, compassion, pride. Joel is a fool.'

*   *   *

Bernardo was expected back in time for the celebration evening meal Miranda had organised that night for Nico's birthday, and consequently Cassie wasn't entirely surprised to come downstairs after lunch and find an unfamiliar young man entering the hall. Both of them paused, studying one another. Bernardo was a younger version of his father, very Italian and very attractive, and a little to her own amusement Cassie felt her skin colouring faintly at the frankly male way his appreciative glance caressed her. Caressed was definitely the word, she mused as she continued downstairs. Bernardo's appreciation made her feel feminine and enticing and she could feel herself responding to the charm of it.

'You must be the Cassie I have heard so much about,' he told her coming to greet her. Cassie held out her hand and smiled, but Bernardo laughed. 'Ah no *cara*, you would not deny me the privilege of greeting a new member of my family in the traditional way?'

Cassie suspected that the way he held her was far from fraternal, as indeed was the way he lingered over kissing her cheek and fingertips. Although not as tall or as broad as Joel and probably a couple of years younger, Bernardo was a very attractive man, and what's more unlike Joel he obviously found her attractive too.

· Both Miranda and Nico were out and so Cassie found herself agreeing to spend the afternoon with Bernardo and bring him up to date on the arrangements for Saturday's party.

He suggested that they discuss them while walking through the villa gardens. 'Our gardens are one of the things I missed most in Brussels,' he told her as they ambled beneath the rose covered trellises.

'So you are married to Miranda's son,' he murmured when Cassie had finished enumerating the delights Miranda had planned for the birthday ball. 'If I were your husband, *cara*, I would not allow you to stay away from me for so long.' The look in his eyes made Cassie's colour fluctuate delicately. It was frankly sensual yet in no way frightening, rather it was extremely intoxicating.

'Joel is extremely busy at the moment,' she responded sedately. 'It was a good opportunity for me to get to know his mother.'

'An idea which certainly did not come from him,' Bernardo commented dryly, a certain irony entering his voice. 'In my memory at least Joel has never made the slightest attempt to concern himself in any way with his mother. This is something that both saddens and angers my father. You know the story of how they met and fell in love while Miranda was still married to Joel's father?'

Cassie agreed that she did.

'Miranda is an honourable woman and one I love very dearly. It is a pity her son cannot see her for the woman she really is, although he does much to redeem himself in my eyes by his choice of a bride.'

The caressing note was back in his voice, and remembering Miranda's teasing comments about flirting she allowed herself to bask in it, and even to respond by saying lightly, 'And by allowing me to visit Miranda on my own . . .'

'By that as well,' Bernardo agreed readily, 'although were you my bride little Cassie, you would not be allowed to venture too far from my arms alone. Indeed were you my wife,' he continued extravagantly, 'I believe I would have to abandon my office duties for a considerable length of time; at least until the sight of you in my bed in the morning did not raise my blood pressure to dangerous levels.' Bernardo laughed openly at Cassie's rich blush.

'Ah, so innocent still. My father was right when he described you as an extremely rare and delicate flower. In Italy we know how to nurture and take care of such things, but somehow I suspect that your Englishman does not.'

Cassie had no wish to be drawn into any unguarded criticisms of Joel or indeed anything that might betray the true state of her marriage to Bernardo. Flirtation was what Miranda had said and Cassie sensed that as long as Bernardo believed her to be happy in her marriage that was all he would indulge in. The problem was, as she readily admitted to herself; she was so unused to the heady intoxication of flattery and male attention that she stood in grave danger of taking it too seriously, of allowing herself to be drawn into something that she might later regret simply for the purpose of flexing her new-found feminine power. An affair with Bernardo pleasant though it might be in many ways, was not really what she wanted and yet, when she looked at him and saw the admiration in his eyes, she couldn't quite help wondering what it would be like to be kissed by him; to be kissed indeed as a man did kiss a woman he found attractive and desirable.

All the kisses she had received had been given in anger, resentment, punishment or just simply out of necessity, and she shivered suddenly, wondering if she would ever find someone to oust Joel from her heart, or if she was destined to spend the rest of her life yearning hopelessly for him. Live for the moment she advised herself, smiling gratefully as Bernardo expressed quick concern that she might be chilly.

'I forget that I am wearing a suit,' he told her, gesturing briefly to the extremely expensive and well-fitting garment he was wearing, 'while you are dressed in no more than a few wisps of silk.'

In point of fact Cassie was wearing a very pretty silk blouse teamed with a toning patterned skirt, but somehow Bernardo's choice of words transformed these attractive but thoroughly respectable garments into something far more provocative and scanty. It was almost as though he already knew of the brief silk undies she was wearing next to her skin, and was indeed pleasurably employed in studying her in them.

Cassie couldn't remember enjoying anything quite as much as Nico's birthday meal. Only the four of them were dining, Miranda having pronounced that since all his family were invited to the ball they could keep just to an intimate foursome without offending anybody.

Nico had been genuinely thrilled with his present, kissing Cassie with affection. Miranda had brought him a small watercolour he had been coveting for some time, and Bernardo's gift to his father was a beautiful antique firearm he had found, he told them, in a small shop in Brussels.

Once the meal was over they sat chatting in the

main salon until Cassie realised with a small start of surprise that it was well past midnight. Excusing herself she stood up.

'Ah *cara*, if only I were your husband,' Bernardo murmured irrepressibly, 'my poor father would never get a report on my progress in Brussels.'

'I think what he means is that were he married to you, he could use you as an excuse for not staying behind to give Nico his reports,' Miranda interpreted. They all laughed, including Bernardo, but Cassie was aware of a glow of pleasure when she prepared for bed that night, that she could seldom remember experiencing before.

Careful Cassie, she warned herself. He's very attractive, but he's also a flirt. So what, a tiny rebellious voice prompted dangerously. Why shouldn't she enjoy Bernardo's flirting; even respond to it a little. It was only a game after all, and so far there had been precious little opportunity for playing in her life. She was a married woman she reminded herself, feeling half guilty and half shocked by her own apparent metamorphosis of character. She had never imagined herself capable of such almost giddy behaviour before. Married yes, but married to a man who despised her; who was more than content to leave her completely alone, and who had already broken any vow of faithfulness he had made to her.

The morning of the ball dawned fair and clear as all mornings in Florence appeared to do, and it passed in a confused bustle of organised chaos with deliveries seeming to arrive every few minutes, and caterers and other temporary staff milling around in the large villa kitchens and formal rooms.

Carlo was coming to the villa in the late afternoon to do their hair, and Cassie now felt confident enough of her own ability to have no nervous fears about her make-up.

Her gown was delivered shortly after lunch. Cassie had barely been able to eat, keyed up by an unanticipated sense of excitement she was loath to admit had anything to do with the admiring, amorous glances Bernardo kept giving her.

'I told you he would fall for you didn't I?' Miranda murmured after lunch. 'He's very attractive isn't he?'

'Very,' Cassie agreed. 'I suspect it's going to my head.' She waited to see what her hostess would make of her admission but Miranda simply laughed and hugged her fondly. 'Oh Cassie, I so much hoped it would. Bernardo is just what you need to provide the final touch of gloss . . . that air a beautiful woman glows with when she knows herself admired and desired. Tonight when Bernardo suggests the two of you walk through the gardens, as I am sure he will . . . go with him . . .'

'And Joel?' Cassie questioned cautiously. She knew what Miranda was saying to her; that she understood her suddenly emergent desire to try her new wings and that she was encouraging her to do so, but there was still Joel, Miranda's son.

'If my son chooses to neglect his wife, and another man tries to steal her from him, he only has himself to blame,' Miranda told her softly.

'Enjoy yourself tonight Cassie. Forget everything but the fact that you are young and beautiful.'

Those words echoed in Cassie's head as she stood in front of her mirror several hours later, trying to match the reflection of herself she now saw in the mirror with the one she remembered from before her visit to Florence. Gone was the dowdy plain girl she remembered and in her place stood a radiant woman, glowing with self-confidence, sure of herself and her femininity.

Signora Tonli had excelled herself with the pale green dress. Tiny puffed sleeves slid artfully down Cassie's arms in line with the discreetly low-cut bosom of her gown. From an almost impossibly small waist the fabric billowed out in a huge full skirt, made up of several layers of the soft green silk stiffened with further layers of stiff underskirts. The topmost layers of green silk were caught up at intervals with tiny bunches of white silk flowers, those same flowers threaded through Cassie's hair, which for the occasion had been pinned up in a soft confusion of curls that emphasised the delicacy of her bone structure and the brilliance of her eyes. Eyes that gleamed almost as green as her dress, she noticed, checking her make-up anxiously. What would Miranda say when she saw her? Would she be pleased? Was she going to look over-dressed? A thousand tiny flutters of panic took flight in her stomach, and Cassie knew that if the door hadn't opened to admit Miranda at that point she would have been in danger of losing all her confidence and refusing to go downstairs.

'Let me look at you.'

Dutifully Cassie twirled round on the delicate

heels of the pale green silk sandals especially made to go with her gown, at the same time admiring Miranda's elegant blue silk.

'A visitation of youth,' Miranda proclaimed half teasingly at last.

'You don't think it's too young for me?' Cassie asked anxiously. 'Miranda I don't . . .'

'Shush, not a word more, it's time we went down. Nico wants you to stand with us as we welcome our guests. That way we can introduce you to everyone.'

It was Cassie's first experience of a truly formal ball but after a while her nervousness disappeared and she found herself able to cope with the many introductions, smiling warmly at the guests, and agreeing that yes, it was a shame her husband could not be with them.

It was eleven o'clock before the last guest arrived. A buffet supper was being served in the long gallery, and Cassie willingly accepted Bernardo's escort there, trying not to blush too hard as he filled her ear with outrageous compliments—and suggestions.

'Ah, tonight you look fresh and innocent enough to be unmarried . . . what a temptation you present . . . the look of innocence coupled with the knowledge of . . .'

'A married woman,' Cassie reminded him repressively. 'I *am* married Bernardo.'

'To a man who has not visited you once in nearly six weeks if my papa is to be believed. What manner of man is this husband of yours *cara*?'

'A very busy one,' Cassie told him dryly, trying not to let pain edge up under the words.

'Too busy for his so lovely wife? When you think no one is looking you have an expression of great unhappiness. Why I wonder? Come,' Bernardo added persuasively, 'you cannot really be hungry—not after that lunch Maria made for us today. Let us walk through the gardens and you can whisper to me what makes you so unhappy.'

On the point of refusing, of reminding him yet again that she was married, Cassie suddenly revolted. Why should she be at such pains to remember her vows; vows which she had given under duress. But she loved Joel, she reminded herself.

'Come *cara*, before some other man steals you from me,' Bernardo begged. 'I am not blind, even if your husband is. You are a very desirable woman Cassie—more girl than woman tonight in that dress—and I do not intend to let one of my father's guests steal you from me.'

The garden had been transformed into a magical wonderland with what appeared to be thousands of coloured lanterns, and Cassie allowed herself to be caught up in the dreamy other-world quality the transformation evoked as Bernardo led her along rose scented paths in the direction of the small sunken garden at the far end of the rose walk.

Private and secluded, Cassie had often reflected as she enjoyed the late afternoon sunshine in it, that the arbour must have been a trysting place for many pairs of lovers throughout the years. Now it was her turn.

She knew that Bernardo was going to kiss her; might even make light love to her, but instead of shying away from him she went readily into his arms, suddenly marvellously soft and pliant, seeming to know with an instinct she hadn't known she possessed, just what to do. His mouth feathered across hers, its warmth pleasant. Cassie closed her eyes automatically and then immediately wished she had not as Joel's dark, hard features took possession of her mind. No matter how much she tried, she could not summon up Bernardo's handsome, boyish face. She could not, she would not think about Joel while Bernardo was kissing her.

'*Cara* . . . what is wrong? Where have you gone?' Bernardo scolded against her mouth. 'You . . .' He broke off abruptly, his arms tensing round her and Cassie immediately opened her eyes. No wonder Bernardo was annoyed with her. There must indeed be something wrong with her, she thought blinking hard, because even with her eyes open all she could see was Joel's hard angry face. It took several seconds for Cassie to realise that he wasn't simply something conjured up by her over-active imagination, but there in the flesh, his eyes hard blue sapphires in the compelling darkness of his face as he watched her with thin-lipped anger.

'Joel . . . what are you doing here?' Even as the words faltered into the tense silence Cassie realised the inanity of them. Bernardo had already released her, and taken a step away from her, as well he might, she thought distractedly gazing at Joel's taller, harder frame.

'I'm beginning to ask myself that same question,' Joel responded in a grating voice. 'I thought I'd come to collect my wife, and to attend a birthday party, but it seems I've only just arrived in time to . . .'

'I shall leave you to your husband *cara*,' Bernardo broke in hastily, 'I must return to the house and my father's guests . . .'

'Yet another faint-hearted cavalier you chose for yourself,' Joel mocked sarcastically when Bernardo had gone. 'Again you're left to face your husband's wrath all alone.'

'Perhaps because he knows there is no reason for you to feel anger,' Cassie responded, thinking of the very brief caress she and Bernardo had shared, and how innocent and tentative it had been compared with Joel's infidelities, but it seemed that Joel had misunderstood her because his mouth tightened, his fingers gripping her arms just below the pretty puff sleeves of her gown.

'So you told him all about our marriage did you Cassie? About your husband, who is not your lover. What a pity I arrived before you had a chance to offer him your virginity, or have you already done so?'

As he bent threateningly towards her Cassie caught the faint smell of alcohol on his breath. Panic beat fiercely inside her increasing the uneven thud of her heart. This was a Joel she did not recognise; his anger had been as cold and cutting as ice, now it possessed all the pent-up force of a volcano on the edge of eruption and she shivered despite the heat of the warm Italian night.

'How did you know where to find me?' she murmured, playing for time, wanting to steer him back to the comparative safety of the house

before he unleashed against her the rage she
could feel burning up inside him.

'My mother told me,' he told her, shocking her
with his announcement. He laughed mirthlessly
when he saw her face. 'So you still possess some
innocence then,' he taunted. 'No doubt she
hoped to torment me with your infidelity the way
she tormented my father with her own.'

'No.' Cassie's denial was immediate and edged
with pain. How could he be so bitter about his
mother, so wrong in his assessment of her?

'I see she has been busy in other directions as
well,' he added slowly, the fingers of one hand
tangling in her soft curls while the other retained
a punishing grip on her arm. The pressure of his
fingers in her hair forced her head back so that he
could inspect her face and body at leisure.
Cassie's skin burned under the explicit exploration of his glance as it slid slowly over her body.

'Umm,' he said at last. 'It seems a pity to waste
so much time and effort wouldn't you say?'

Not a word about her changed appearance
Cassie thought furiously, not a single comment
on how she looked, just that cold assessing
scrutiny. She opened her mouth to give voice to
her anger and almost reeled with shock as her
parted lips were covered by the hard heat of
Joel's, his grip on her hair forcing her head back
until she thought her neck would snap. It was no
tentative, explorative kiss such as she had
expected to share with Bernardo, but a fiercely
sexual statement made by a man who wanted to
stamp his mark of possession so clearly on her
that it would stay with her for all her life. Cassie
swayed into his body, clutching the front of his

jacket, too shocked to resist as his tongue probed the soft interior of her mouth, his teeth bruising the soft inner skin of her lips.

Joel's hand left her hair and slid down her back pressing her into him until her hands were trapped between their bodies, and she could feel the fierce beat of his heart. His mouth left her lips to explore the angle of her jaw, and the delicate curve of her throat. Fierce waves of pleasure exploded inside her, and unconsciously Cassie arched tentatively against him, her arms locking round him.

'Cassie, Joel, are you there? We're just about to cut the cake.'

The sound of Miranda's voice calling their names brought Cassie back down to earth. At the same moment as she tensed Joel released her, stepping back into the shadows so that she couldn't read his expression.

'Come on,' he told her abruptly, 'We'd better get back.'

CHAPTER EIGHT

'I STILL don't understand how Joel knew it was Nico's birthday,' Cassie remarked in confusion, filling her coffee cup and wrapping her fingers round it.

She and Miranda were alone in the villa. Nico had gone out with Bernardo, and Joel was staying at an hotel in Florence itself.

'I wrote and told him,' Miranda told her placidly. 'Don't you see, Cassie,' she explained wryly, 'I knew it would give him an excuse to come and get you without it being seen that he was giving in. Men are like that, my dear; very vulnerable through their pride. We women are far more practical.'

'In other words you want to get rid of me,' Cassie said half wondering if it was true.

Miranda's expression reassured her that it was not. 'My dear girl you know that is not the case. Were it possible I would keep you here with me as long as I could, but that would be selfish of me. Your place is with Joel. He is your husband.'

'For the next few months at least,' Cassie agreed dryly. 'He didn't even comment on how I looked,' she added thoughtfully, not aware that her eyes clouded as she spoke. 'I don't believe he even noticed.'

'He noticed all right,' Miranda assured her. 'You sent him out into the garden deliberately, didn't you?' Cassie questioned her chidingly, 'Knowing that I'd be with Bernardo?'

Miranda smiled ruefully, 'I thought the hint of a little competition might stir him up a little.'

Cassie smiled sadly to herself. She knew that Miranda had hoped to make Joel jealous. Miranda still had hopes that somehow their mock marriage could be transformed into a real one, but Cassie had banished that foolish dream when she looked into Joel's eyes in the garden and read nothing but contempt for her in them. True he had kissed her, but more as a punishment than anything else.

'After all he is taking you home with him,' Miranda pointed out.

'Because he needs me as hostess for this party he is giving to celebrate the "merger" of our two companies,' Cassie pointed out dryly.

This had been something Joel had explained to her before leaving her the previous evening. Although the news of their marriage had done much to restore confidence in his own business venture, he had decided that a cocktail party to celebrate both their marriage and their 'merger' would help to further gild the lily, and he wanted Cassie there to act as his hostess.

They were flying back to London later that afternoon. Joel had been curt with his mother and distant almost to the point of rudeness to Nico on the night of the party, and Cassie sighed, remembering the pain she had seen in Miranda's eyes when she looked at him.

By lunch-time she was packed and waiting. Joel arrived an hour later, looking as grim and uncompromising as ever. Cassie hugged Miranda warmly, tearful now that the moment of parting had come.

'Remember,' Miranda whispered to her, 'whatever happens, there'll always be a bond between us, Cassie. After all we both love the same person don't we?'

Joel had loaded her cases into the car while Cassie said her goodbyes, with a brief nod to his mother he helped Cassie into the car.

'Why the woebegone face,' he demanded as he drove away. 'Missing your Italian Romeo already are you?'

Cassie knew he meant Bernardo but she said nothing, simply firming her lips and staring resolutely out of her window.

The flight back to Heathrow was uneventful, and apart from feeling rather tired, Cassie felt no other emotions about returning to her native soil.

She had half expected Joel to make some excuse to remain in London while she returned to the house, but he did not.

It was late evening before they reached Howard Court. Exhausted by a full day's travelling Cassie noticed blearily as she stepped into the hall that the decorators had finished and that the room now glowed softly as it must have done in the days when Miranda was mistress, but all she really wanted to do was to have a warm bath and go to bed. Time enough to inspect the house in the morning. A little to her surprise Joel had announced that the cocktail party was to be held here and not in London. That was something else she would have to sort out, she thought wearily, walking upstairs, but fortunately she felt more than equal to that task now, after staying with Miranda.

'Cassie.'

Joel's cool voice halted her progress upstairs. She turned, and frowned down at him.

'Fancy a nightcap?'

Cassie shook her head, telling herself she must be imagining the brief look of disappointment that crossed his face. A trick of the light no doubt she reflected tiredly as she walked into her room. Joel had no desire for her company; no desire for her full-stop.

In the morning he had gone. Cassie found a note from him in the kitchen explaining that he was needed in London and that his secretary would be in touch with her with a prospective guest list for the party.

The decorators had more than lived up to their reputation, and the soft furnishings and carpets glowed softly after their cleaning. Before she left Italy Miranda had given her several messages for Mary Jensen and Cassie decided to walk down to the vicarage to pass them on.

Mary smiled her pleasure when she opened the door to Cassie. 'My goodness you do look well,' she pronounced, 'and so very pretty.'

'Miranda's work,' Cassie told her ruefully, 'she's been polishing me up. I'm afraid in this case my "beauty" is definitely only a surface gloss.'

'Nonsense,' Mary told her stoutly, 'I thought myself what an attractive girl you could be if you only took a little trouble. You've far too low an opinion of yourself Cassie. Now come and tell me all about Miranda,' she invited, 'and about Italy.'

It was over an hour before Cassie left, and she
let herself back into the house to find the 'phone
ringing imperiously. She picked up the receiver
and found Joel's secretary on the other end of the
line.

Her purpose in ringing was to discuss the
cocktail party which was to be held in a
fortnight's time, and Cassie, who had previously
found herself rather in awe of her, was surprised
how easy she found it to discuss the relative
merits of respective caterers.

'Joel normally uses a Mayfair firm,' his
secretary told her, 'but perhaps you ...' She
paused tactfully, and Cassie hastily assured her
that she had no personal preferences, 'Although I
should like to see sample menus,' she told her.

Whether it was because she now had more self-
confidence herself she did not know but Cassie
found the girl far more responsive and pleasant to
her. She promised to send Cassie a list of the
invitees and they arranged that Cassie would go
up to London in person as soon as it could be
arranged so that they could go through the
organisation together.

The rest of the day seemed to be spent in
organising flowers and drink, in making arrangements for Mrs Pollit to work on the day of the
party. She must also check to see how many
people would want accommodation overnight,
Cassie reflected, making a list as she went along.

It was evening before she managed to find any
time to spend on her own work, but it was hard
to concentrate when with every breath she was
listening for sounds of Joel's return.

It was late when he did come back. Cassie was

already in bed. She lay tensely against the mattress listening to the sounds of him moving about. She fell asleep before he came upstairs and in the morning when she got up he had gone again. So much for his mother's hopes, she thought a little bitterly, only admitting to herself then how much she had hoped that her transformed appearance would elicit a response from him. But then Joel was used to attractive, even beautiful women, and he knew what she was like beneath the surface gloss Miranda had applied. It was hardly to be expected that he would want her, she told herself. The only time they actually met as equals was when they talked about their respective businesses. She found Joel's work especially fascinating and liked the fact that he talked to her about it as he would have done to any knowledgeable colleague. It was their only common ground Cassie thought sadly as she worked on her own project, hardly the basis for building a marriage on. But then Joel didn't want to build their marriage; he didn't want to be married to her at all.

She had just managed to dam her destructively depressing thoughts and concentrate on her work when she heard a car coming up the drive. A glance at her watch showed her that it was much later than she had realised, but still early for Joel to be returning home. She walked into the hall at the same moment he unlocked the front door, and Cassie was shocked by the white pallor of his face.

She started to speak but fell silent as he told her curtly, 'Migraine . . . don't fuss. I've got some pills upstairs . . .'

Cassie's father had suffered the curse of

migraine and she well knew how Joel must be
feeling.

While he went upstairs she hurried into the
kitchen to make him a drink, freezing as she
heard a crash from upstairs.

She found him in the bathroom off his
bedroom, leaning against the basin, tiny shards of
glass all around him. His skin looked like putty,
his eyes for once drained of all colour, almost
black.

'It's only the water glass,' he told her, spacing
the words carefully as though even to speak
caused him the most unendurable agony. 'Leave
it, I'll . . .'

'You'll go and lie down,' Cassie told him
firmly, taking command. 'Are these your pills?'
She picked up the small bottle beside the basin,
and Joel nodded.

Quickly reading the instructions Cassie shook
out two and handed them to him, watching him
grimace as he swallowed them quickly.

'Go and lie down,' she repeated, 'I'm just
making you a hot drink. I'll clear this up when I
come back.'

She was gone about five minutes and half
expected to find Joel asleep when she returned,
because the tablets he had been prescribed were
strong ones, but when she walked into his
bedroom he was lying on the bed, his eyes closed
and his body tense.

Automatically Cassie closed the curtains,
seeing him shudder as a ray of evening sunshine
fell across his closed eyes.

'Try and drink this,' she urged him sitting
down beside him and automatically helping him

to lift his head. 'It will make the tablets work faster.'

'You seem to know a lot about it?' His voice was slurred, more by the pain than anything else, Cassie suspected, studying the pupils of his eyes.

'My father suffered from migraine. The only thing that seemed to help was a neck massage. It seemed to relieve a lot of the tension ...' a thought struck her. 'Would you like me to see if it will work for you?'

'Anything to get rid of this damned pain,' Joel grunted. 'It started just after lunch. I should have stopped then, but I had too much to do.'

'You should have stayed in London instead of driving home,' Cassie scolded, deftly unfastening his tie and slipping the top buttons of his shirt free, before gently pushing him back on to the bed.

'Perhaps I wanted to get home to the loving ministrations of my wife,' she thought she heard him say, but his words were muffled slightly by the pillow and in any case she was concentrating on easing his shirt away from the back of his neck without exacerbating the pain.

'Take the damn thing off.' This time there was no mistaking his demand. He lifted his head slightly from the pillow, his face even paler than it had been before. She could see the pain darkening his eyes and didn't waste time talking, simply quickly unfastening the remaining shirt buttons, and tugging it free of his trousers as gently as she could, before easing it off his body.

The moment she had it free he flopped back against the mattress. Cassie had performed this task many times for her father when he had been suffering from the same complaint, but the curious dryness in her throat reminded her that this was not her father lying in front of her; that the sunbronzed sleekly muscled back and dark thick hair did not belong to her parent but to the man she loved. Steeling herself not to betray her feelings Cassie flexed her fingers and reached out across the bed. Because of its width it strained her back to reach so far, and slipping off her shoes she climbed on to the mattress kneeling beside Joel.

He gave no sign of being aware of her presence, his breathing sharp and shallow as though even that pained him. Flexing her fingers again, and forcing herself to empty her mind of everything other than his pain Cassie stroked her fingers along the line of his collar bone, thumbs investigating the flesh of his back, searching for tension points. The betraying hard lump just below his neck told its own story and she started to massage it slowly, knowing it had been caused by tension; the same tension that was no doubt responsible for his present headache.

For several minutes there were no sounds in the room other than those of their mingled breathing, Joel's slightly deeper and more relaxed now and conversely her own more shallow, betraying the effect touching him was having on her senses.

Her fingers stroked their way up his neck finding and soothing the tensely corded muscles, experience making it possible for her to continue her task without giving in to the insidious pull of her senses.

She paused once, feeling herself shake with

tension, using as an excuse the drink she had made for him. He drank it obediently, the pupils of his eyes slightly enlarged. The drug must be starting to take effect Cassie decided as he flopped back against the bed.

This time when her fingers touched his skin Cassie could feel the tension easing away, his breathing was more relaxed, and she felt the corded muscles respond to her touch.

'No, don't stop,' Joel demanded thickly when she moved away slightly flexing her tense spine. 'It feels good.'

She doubted that he knew what he was saying, but it gave her the excuse she needed to let her hands explore the firm contours of his back, an exploration that was pure self indulgence—and dangerous with it, she chided herself as his breathing deepened and he gave a small groan of pleasure as she stroked the tension from his spine. His skin was warm, faintly moist, his muscles supple, and she ached with a tension she knew had nothing to do with over-work. She loved him so much Cassie acknowledged, shivering under the impact of the admission, and yet every ounce of logic she possessed warned her of the dangers of allowing herself to love anyone, never mind someone who was so obviously indifferent to her. Her fingers stilled and she started to move away. Joel turned over, his eyes closed, his skin no longer quite as pale. Fine dark hairs patterned his chest, arrowing downwards over his flat stomach. Her heart flipped over and formed a hard lump in her chest, longing and anguish mingling in a wave of intense pain. His fingers curled round her wrist as she sat back on her heels without touching him, his eyes still closed as he murmured blurrily, 'Stay with me . . . I want you to stay with me . . .'

He didn't want *her* at all of course. Cassie doubted that he even knew who she was. What he wanted was the comfort her skilled fingers had transmitted to his tense body, and his tired, drug-hazed mind confused that need with something totally different, but as his fingers closed tightly round her wrist, Cassie found herself giving in to the pressure he was exerting and allowing herself to be pulled down to lie alongside him on the double bed. Stiff and tense, her breathing spasmodic and jerky, it seemed to cease altogether when Joel's arm curled round her, welding her to his side, his head burrowing against her breasts and pillowing itself there.

Through the thin stuff of her blouse she could feel his breath warming her skin. His arm was wrapped round her waist, and as he tugged her downwards her skirt had wrapped itself round her thighs. Its button fastening dug painfully into her side. Cassie lay still for a few seconds telling herself she would move once Joel was properly asleep but when she eventually did try to move she found that it was impossible. The weight of his head against her breasts pinned her to the bed, and she couldn't move without disturbing him. His arm held her tightly against him and as she made a tentative movement to dislodge it he muttered protestingly in his sleep, tightening his hold on her.

Her skin tingled from the heat of his breath. Her efforts to move had pulled the top two buttons at the vee necked fastening of her shirtblouse free and exposed the delicate lace of her bra—one of the new ones Miranda had chosen for her. The buttons on her skirt still dug into her waist and gingerly Cassie reached round and managed to unfasten them, telling herself that she would stay where she was for a little while longer and then find some way of moving away.

Closing her eyes she gave in to daydreams, letting her imagination pretend that she and Joel were in actual fact lovers; that she was in his arms because he could not bear to let her go, rather than because he had turned to her simply for warmth and comfort. His breathing, slow and soft now, fluttered her pulses into erotic awareness, a pleasurable lassitude relaxed her body until it melted against his. Her eyes closed and Cassie's fingers found and stroked through the dark hair at the back of Joel's head. She would go in a few minutes . . . just a few minutes.

Cassie was dreaming and it was the most delightful dream imaginable. Joel was making love to her, his hands and lips stroking and caressing her body into molten pleasure. She murmured his name in a small throaty purr, revelling in the warmth of his mouth against her skin, free from the need to hide how she felt from him; free to touch and caress him as he was caressing her. Her fingers stroked along his spine as she felt the warmth of his mouth probing the valley between her breasts. Her bones had turned to liquid; she was completely formless, floating free in a deliciously euphoric state which pushed aside the bonds of reality. Joel's hand moved,

seeking the impediment that prevented his mouth
from savouring the soft roundness of her breasts
and Cassie moved eagerly to assist him, filled
with an exquisite rush of pleasure as his lips
feathered delicately against her nipple, his hand
cupping her breast and then caressing it as
delicate exploration started to give way to
passion.

It was her own gasp of mingled delight and
hunger that woke Cassie to reality and to the
discovery that Joel's caresses were no dream. In
the darkness of the room she could just make out
the contours of his face, his eyes closed in
passionate concentration as his mouth moved
against her body. Intense spears of pleasure
hurtled through her body, mind battling against
desire and losing in the wild surge of pleasure
flooding through her. Joel's hand left her breast,
caressing the curve of her waist, pushing aside
her skirt to stroke along her hip, a deep sound of
pleasure murmured against her skin as his body
sought closer contact with hers.

Cassie knew she should wake him up; knew
that his actions were instinctive, simple reactions
to her proximity; that he had no idea who he was
making love to, but she couldn't stop herself from
sliding her fingers down his spine; from exploring
the shape of the muscles that lay beneath his skin
and from following the arrowing of dark hair up
over his chest, to accidently brush across the hard
flatness of his nipple and feel its unexpected
response to her touch. Her fingers lingered,
exploring delicately, surprised by his physical
response. His lips tightened over her nipple, his
fingers curling into her hip. Immediately Cassie

removed her fingers, trembling slightly in shock and desire. She hadn't known men could be so physically responsive to so small a caress, and she was half ashamed of her own deep seated urge to go on to elicit from him an intensity of desire that would push aside the barriers of restraint, but even as she drew away his mouth slid to the hollow between her breasts, his voice thick and slurred as he groaned. 'No ... don't stop ... touch me again ...'

Cassie looked wildly down at him, wondering if he realised who she was. His eyes were still closed and she suspected he was still half asleep, still under the influence of the pain-killing drug, but his lips were teasing tormenting kisses against her breasts, his fingers exploring the satin smoothness of her stomach, turning her body to fiery liquid, making it shudder with pleasure and need.

She reached out, touching him tentatively again and then growing bolder as he made husky sounds of pleasure against her skin, his tongue stroking nerve sensitising circles of delight around her now gently swollen breasts. When it flicked against their hardened tips, tormenting them with the promise of pleasures to come she felt all self-control slipping away from her. Her hands stroked feverishly over Joel's skin, her lips pressing wild, impassioned kisses against the smooth flesh of his shoulder, a small moaning cry of passion wrung from her lips as his teeth grated achingly over the taut fullness of her breast.

Without being able to do a thing to stop herself Cassie found she was arching wantonly against him, needing the hard thrust of his hips against her lower body, her fingers sliding into his hair as he tugged avidly at the centre of her breast until pleasure became almost a pain and she was forced to cry out, shaking with the intensity of her own emotion and the physical hunger she sensed building up inside him.

She knew instantly that Joel was now awake, and tensed against his rejection, shivering with shame that she should have so betrayed herself. Unable to look at him she started to move away, only to find herself imprisoned between his hands, his hoarse, 'No . . .' stunning her into stillness as he raised his head to look into her eyes and then still looking at her deliberately bent his head to feather warm, moist lips across the tensed outline of her own, wooing them into tenuous response.

'Make love with me Cassie.' He whispered the words against her mouth interspersing them with gentle kisses, soothing her as though he knew all her fears, and even though she knew she would regret what she was doing Cassie found herself responding, touching the smooth skin of his shoulder, pressing her lips against it in obedience to his husky command, quivering against him as he rolled her beneath him pinning her with the weight of his thighs, his fingers cupping and stroking the tender fullness of her breast as though he knew how it still ached from the exquisite agony caused by the heated pressure of his mouth.

One part of her still refused to believe what was happening, even when Joel moved her slightly to ease away her skirt completely. That was probably why she did and said nothing when he pulled off his own clothes, her eyes widening over the darkness-dimmed outline of his body, her cheeks burning as she felt the unmistakable contraction of her lower stomach in response to his masculinity.

'Sweet Cassie, did I hurt you?' Cassie heard him murmur throatily as his thumb probed the crest of her breast still tender and slightly sore. 'Shall I make it better?' He bent his head feathering light, moist caresses around the throbbing aureol before she could say anything, one hand spread possessively over the curve of her hip while the other held and caressed her other breast.

Shivers of molten pleasure inflamed her skin, sensations so alien and intense that they half frightened her, taking hold of her body. Her nails dug protestingly into Joel's back as his tongue rasped over the soreness of her nipple, and then pain gave way to unbelievable surges of pleasure causing her to arch feverishly against him, and welcome the tight coiling urgency occasioned by the fierce demand of his mouth against her tender skin.

After that there was no turning back. In a dream Cassie followed with wondering eyes and pulsing senses the erotic path of Joel's mouth against her skin, tensing abruptly in sudden panic when his fingers probed the edge of her briefs.

'Cassie, I want you. Kiss me . . . touch me . . .' Joel's hands urged hers against his body, inciting her to a wanton exploration of his maleness that made him shudder and mutter her name into her skin. Excitement spiralled up inside her as she registered his hectic response, her lips explored the smooth column of his throat, wondering at the tension in his body as he arched beneath her gentle touch, inciting her to explore further; to discover that the hard male nipples were almost as responsive as her own, too excited by Joel's feverish response to her to be aware that he had removed her briefs. until she felt his fingers cupping the rounded softness of her bottom, lifting her against him.

'Cassie . . .' Her name was a long drawn out moan of need and she shivered involuntarily, tense with a mixture of love and fear.

'Joel . . .' She wanted to tell him that she loved him, but his mouth against hers dammed the words, her body convulsed by totally unexpected waves of pleasure as his fingers caressed her intimately, the soft words of praise he murmured against her ear coaxing her trembling body to relax and accept the male thrust of his.

His mouth caught her faint cry of pain, silencing it, his body responsive to her sudden tension, gentling it until Cassie felt a renewed surge of pleasure, which she knew was echoed by Joel's body.

Eager now to please him and give him the same degree of pleasure he was giving her, her hands caressed the lean contours of his body, her mouth exploring the rigid muscles of his throat.

'Cassie.' He gasped her name as though in pain, twining his fingers into her hair as he twisted her mouth under his own and drank deeply from it, shuddering beneath the deep surges of pleasure rocking both their bodies.

Later Cassie remembered him looking at her

afterwards and starting to say something, but she was already on the verge of sleep, too exhausted both emotionally and physically to hear what he was saying.

CHAPTER NINE

SHE woke up in the morning slowly, conscious of a pleasurable lassitude and numerous small aches that made her face colour at the memory of how they had been caused. She was alone in Joel's bed and at first she thought he had left the house, but as she rolled over, burying her face in his pillow and breathing the scent of him into her lungs she heard sounds from the adjoining bathroom. She had no time to move before Joel emerged, a brief towel wrapped round his hips, his hair wet from his shower.

For a few seconds they simply looked at one another, Cassie focusing blindly on Joel's bare shoulder, unable to meet his eyes, deeply ashamed of her responses to him and frightened of what he might read into them. She couldn't endure his scorn; his mocking comparison of her clumsy attempts to please him with the more skilled embraces of his customary lovers. Neither could she survive hearing him say he had guessed her secret. Too late now for 'if onlys', she could only keep on staring at him until he drawled succinctly, 'Stop looking at it as though you don't remember how it got there, Cass, those marks were caused by your teeth, my little wife, and the scratches on my back by your nails.'

Until that moment she hadn't even noticed the tiny betraying mark on his shoulder, now she did so, her skin colouring vulnerably as she looked hurriedly away. There were marks on her own skin, faint bruises on her arms and even her breasts and she shivered, longing to be anywhere but here. Joel had lived through moments like these far too many times for them to occasion him any embarrassment but she . . .

Pain lodged in her throat, a tight hard lump of misery, tears stinging the backs of her eyes. How could she have been so stupid, wilfully careless of her pride. Surely now Joel must guess how she felt about him. In an agony of mortification she caught back a sob, knowing that her eyes were filling with stupid . . . stupid tears. She lowered her lashes, but it was too late. Tears quivered against them, diamond bright in the morning sunshine.

'Cassie . . .' Joel was frowning, striding towards her. Another moment and he would reach the bed; tell her that what had happened last night had been no fault of his; that he hadn't realised who he had in his arms; that she ought to have woken him; to have stopped him before things had got out of hand.

'No . . .' The moan of pain she gave echoed sharply round the room, stopping Joel where he stood, his frown deepening. 'No . . . I don't want to talk about it,' she told him thickly. 'I . . .' The 'phone rang sharply and clamorously and Joel glared at it, his attention momentarily distracted. Sensing his indecision Cassie muttered thickly, 'You'd better answer it, it might be important.'

Even as he turned his back on her to reach for the receiver, she was sliding out of his bed, not bothering to gather up her clothes—she could retrieve them later. She felt him turn as she raced for the door, her skin flushing as she felt him study her nudity, but refusing to turn round or stop in response to his angry, 'Cassie, wait, I . . .'

In the sanctuary of her own room she locked both her bedroom and her bathroom door, filling the bath with hot water and soaking in it while she tried to come to terms with the turmoil of her thoughts. Could it really be possible that last night she and Joel had been lovers? That he had caressed her body into a mindless whirlpool of desire until she wanted nothing but his complete possession? That he had aroused her to such an extent that she had wanted to touch and caress him with a need nearly as intense as her desire for him. Shame scorched her cheeks. It was one thing to love him in the secret recesses of her heart, it was another to give in weakly to that love; to let it merge with physical desire to the point where her pride and self respect meant nothing and his possession everything, even while she knew how little he really thought of her.

She lingered in the safety of her rooms until she was sure he had gone, refusing to answer the 'phone when she finally did emerge from them just in case he was on the other end of the line. It was the end now. It must be. He wouldn't want to keep on with the pretence of their marriage now. He would probably have guessed her secret and be terrified she might try to force him to remain married to her. Cassie's heart thudded in a mixture of terror and joy as she realised that she might now have a very valid reason for persuading him to continue their marriage. She might already be carrying his child.

If she was she would rear it alone, she decided stoutly, wondering why she was suddenly crying again. In order to distract herself she tried to study the guest list Joel's secretary had sent her for the cocktail party. The Williams' name was included on it Cassie noted with surprise, jumping nervously as the 'phone started to ring again. She ignored it, continuing to scrutinise the list, and then pacing tensely round the study. She ought to do some work, but she felt too tense. She knew she ought to have something to eat, but the thought of food was totally nauseating. Suddenly she longed for Miranda, and stared desperately at the telephone, finally deciding against ringing her. Miranda would guess from her voice that something was wrong and she would worry about her, Cassie knew. It would be selfish of her to add to Miranda's unhappiness over her son.

At three o'clock Cassie finally sat down in front of her computer, a mug of coffee beside her. She had barely started work when she heard a car. Tensing automatically she glanced at the door, and then tried to relax. If it was Joel there was nothing to be gained by running away. She would just have to face whatever it was he had to say.

Her face was white with strain when he finally walked into the study, her fingers interlocked in tight pain beneath her desk.

'Why haven't you been answering the 'phone?'

'I was busy,' she lied, 'working ... I ...' She risked a look at him, and then looked quickly away. His eyes glittered darkly as they studied her face. He too looked tense, probably because he was wondering how to deal with her, Cassie acknowledged miserably.

'Cassie, about last night,' he began, and if she

hadn't known better she could have believed there was anxiety and a certain element of pleading in the way he said the words. Tension coiled through her as she anticipated his rejection. 'I'd rather not talk about it,' she said tersely. 'It happened, and I know we both regret it. If you want me to leave . . .'

'No.' His curt denial startled her for a second, hope flaring brilliantly and ridiculously inside her, only to die immediately as he added. 'You can't—the cocktail party—remember?'

The cocktail party, of course. Stupidly she wanted to laugh, but her throat locked back the sound, her voice high and strained as she agreed, 'Yes . . . I'd forgotten that for the moment . . .'

'I think the best thing would be for me to move out—It shouldn't occasion too much comment. We're very busy at the moment and it isn't unusual for me to stay in London. I'll have to come back for the party of course . . .'

'Of course . . .' Cassie echoed numbly. No doubt he considered himself safe from her love for him for the odd night, especially when they would be surrounded by others.

'Cassie . . .'

She turned her back on him so that he wouldn't see her misery. 'Cassie, if you . . .'

Pride made her fling desperately at him. 'I don't want anything from you, Joel, anything at all . . . except to be left alone to get on with my work.'

Her head was bent over it when the door slammed behind him, but tears blinded her vision. She didn't move until she heard him drive away, his car roaring angrily down the drive. No doubt tonight the woman in his arms would be experienced and safe; unlike herself, she thought bitterly.

Later that night, too strung up to sleep, but knowing that in reality she was tired, she made her way upstairs. Some masochistic impulse directed her footsteps to Joel's room. Drawers and cupboards were half open, mute testimony of his desire to escape, and she moved automatically, picking things up and putting them away, studiously avoiding looking at his bed. It was still rumpled from their joint occupation, his shirt discarded on the floor.

The moment she touched it Cassie knew it was a mistake. The tears started to flow down her face, her body aching with a hunger she now knew was born of her love for him. His scent clung to the soft cotton, and she shuddered as she looked at his bed, torn by a longing to curl up in it and make believe it was last night and he was still here. Wadding the shirt into a tight ball, she threw it into her own laundry basket, knowing that the scent of her own clothes would mask the elusive masculine odour clinging to it. In her bathroom she showered, ignoring the faint bruises on her skin, and pulled on one of her old fashioned cotton nightdresses. Alone in her bed she refused to allow herself to think about him, and then lay sleepless and dry-eyed stoically enduring the pain of loving him and knowing that she wasn't loved in return.

One day slid into ten and Cassie was thankful that she had the preparations for the cocktail party to occupy at least some of her thoughts.

The discovery that she was not to have Joel's
child had been both a relief and a disappointment.
Logically she knew she would want a child of
hers to grow up sure of the love between its
parents, and yet there would have been a special
sweet pain in knowing she had conceived his
child.

The day before the party Joel returned home,
brusque and tired looking. Cassie did everything
she could to appear normal and relaxed, asking
him about the progress with his new development
over dinner.

His replies were curt, his manner preoccupied,
and Cassie caught him looking at her frowningly
on several occasions, studying her as though he
was trying to work something out. Had he
guessed how she felt about him? Cassie's heart
thudded tremulously. If so she prayed he would
not torment her with his knowledge.

'Have you heard from my mother since you left
Florence?' His question startled her. It was the
first time he had ever mentioned Miranda of his
own volition and Cassie responded eagerly,
offering to show him the letter she had received
that morning.

'No thanks,' he responded coldly. 'Has your
Italian Romeo written to you as well?'

Cassie had heard nothing from Bernardo nor
expected to. She knew that there was a tentative
possibility that Bernardo might become engaged
to the daughter of a friend of Nico's because
Miranda had mentioned it to her but she had
heard nothing from Bernardo himself.

'No.' Her reply was as cold as his had been,
and it seemed for a second that his face paled, the

harsh outline of his cheekbones thrown into relief—his expression sombre and withdrawn. The need to reach out and touch him played havoc with her senses and Cassie rushed into speech to try and conceal her emotions. 'Everything's organised for tomorrow,' she told him breathlessly. 'Have you had any problems with the funding for your new research?'

'Why the concern, or is it simply that you want to know when you can expect to be free of me?' He practically snarled the words at her, pushing aside his plate and standing up. 'I've got some work to do, if you'll excuse me.'

Why should he think she wished to be free of him, Cassie wondered, puzzled by the deep vein of anger she had sensed behind his words. Did he genuinely believe she wanted to be free of their marriage or was he simply exercising tact, and easing the burden on her pride by allowing her to think that he did? Either way it was hardly a subject on which she could question him more deeply.

It was harder to sleep that night than ever, knowing that Joel was in the house with her, alone in his bed as she was alone in hers. Reminding herself that tomorrow would be a busy day Cassie tried to relax into sleep, but her dreams were fragmented by tormenting memories of Joel's lovemaking and she woke up unrefreshed and muzzy.

The day passed in a ceaseless whirl of activity. The flowers arrived and she arranged them. Mrs Pollit turned up on time and set about giving the drawing room and the long gallery a final polish. After lunch the caterers arrived. The party was

due to commence at seven and Cassie had been
pleased to hear that none of the guests would be
staying overnight.

At six she made a final check of the rooms, and
inspected the buffet, before going upstairs to get
ready. She had driven into town in the morning
to have her hair styled and it curled softly on to
her shoulders, shining almost chestnut in the
early evening sunlight.

The silk suit she had decided to wear was one
she had bought in Italy, lovely rich golds and
deep blues that added colour and depth to her
eyes, the elegant lines of the silk emphasising her
slender curves.

At six-forty-five she was ready, trying to quell
the nervous flutters of dread in her stomach, and
wondering where Joel was as she went back
downstairs. He emerged from his room, just as
she reached the hall and leaned over the
banister, calling to her impatiently, 'Cassie, can
you help me with this damned cufflink?'

He was wearing dark trousers that clung tautly
to his thighs, his shirt open across the chest.
Slowly Cassie walked back upstairs, trying to
control her breathing, hoping she was equal to
the task of touching him without betraying how
she felt about him.

He extended one lean wrist as she drew level
with him and her fingertips brushed the dark
hairs growing over it. It was all she could do not
to pull away, reminded as she was of the feel of
his chest beneath her fingertips.

'What's the matter?' Joel demanded harshly.
'Can't you even bear to touch me now? You sang
a different tune not so very long ago, Cassie.'

He must have felt her involuntary withdrawal, because lean fingers grasped her chin, his eyes darkly bitter as they studied her strained expression. Quite what he would have said Cassie didn't know, but the peal of the door bell stopped him. He frowned as she turned away, and remembering why he had wanted her, Cassie quickly secured the errant link before hurrying back downstairs, to greet the first arrivals.

A hectic hour-and-a-half followed. Cassie had carefully memorised as many of the names on the guest list as she could; some were familiar to her from the financial press, and with Joel at her side to smooth the introductions she found herself beginning to relax a little as she responded pleasantly to questions about how they had met, and the success of her company.

Once everyone had arrived she and Joel circulated separately and Cassie became involved in a group which included Peter Williams. She was listening to someone talking about the difficulties of finding new and challenging computer games when she remembered that she had not locked her desk drawer, something she always did when she was working on a new game. Excusing herself she hurried into the study, removing her desk key from the small pot beside her computer terminal.

She was just about to lock her desk when she heard the study door opening behind her. Thinking it was Joel she didn't turn round until she felt a hand on her shoulder, her senses telling her instantly that it did not belong to her husband. When she turned round it was Peter Williams who stood in front of her.

'Working on something new, Cassie?' he enquired curiously, his glance sliding from her face to the closed desk drawer. 'Strange how things work out isn't it? If I hadn't been so reluctant to take you to bed no doubt that new game would have been money in my pocket and not Howard's. You've even turned out to be quite a little beauty.' His arm slid round her as he spoke and Cassie froze instinctively. Peter had obviously been drinking and she wasn't sure he was entirely sober. Bitterness and weakness scored unattractive lines alongside his mouth. How could she ever have contemplated marrying him, she wondered looking at him, even to save Cassietronics?

'Come on, you can't tell me that Howard will miss one kiss? After all you owe me that much, Cassie.' His hot breath fanned her cheek and Cassie tensed against a wave of nausea, longing to be free of him and yet sensing that to fight would be to only exacerbate her situation.

She was just about to ask Peter to set her free when the study door opened again but Cassie's initial flood of relief was superceded by a sharp pang of fear as she recognised the anger in Joel's expression.

Peter had obviously seen it too because he released her straight away. 'It wasn't my fault,' he whined backing away. 'She invited me in here, Howard . . . Said she wanted to show me the new game she was working on.' Peter laughed nastily, 'Perhaps she's regretting marrying you already umm? You should have waited for me, darling instead of rushing headlong into marriage with someone else . . .'

'Get out.' Joel held open the door and Peter half lurched through it, turning to give Cassie a bitter smile before Joel slammed the door closed.

'You just couldn't resist it could you?' he demanded, advancing on her. 'You're all the same ... just like my mother ... One man isn't enough for you. Well if you think I'm going to stand idly by and let you take Williams as a lover ... betraying me the way my mother betrayed my father ... Is that why you stayed with me the other night, Cassie ... Let me take your virginity ... because you knew you couldn't dangle Williams on a string much longer without letting him become your lover ... because like my mother ... you wanted the insurance of a legal father for any b ...'

The sharp cracking sound of Cassie's palm against his lean cheek silenced the bitter stream of invective. Her skin stung from the hard contact with his and she was breathing heavily. Violence was something she abhorred and yet she had had to stop him ... stop him before he could accuse her any further. She felt almost physically ill that he could even think such things never mind practically accuse her of them, and for one mad moment she contemplated telling him the truth, but then sanity intruded. Although adult, Joel was still suffering from the wounds his father had inflicted on him as a child, and was beyond comprehending reason or logic, and yet why should he continue to denigrate his mother and her whole sex, when in reality ... She looked up at him and found him glaring furiously back at her, breathing harshly, the red imprint of her hand slowly fading from his skin. The blow had probably hurt her more than it had him and yet she had an overpowering urge to reach out and smooth away the red marks; to place her lips to his skin and . . .

Pushing away the thought Cassie said huskily, 'Joel, you're quite wrong. Both about me and about your mother. Peter followed me in here—I don't know why, you may believe that or otherwise as you choose, I won't make any other explanations or apologies because I don't consider them necessary . . .'

'So I'm wrong about Miranda am I?' Joel taunted her. 'And how did you come to that conclusion . . . what lies has she been telling you, Cassie, what sob-story . . . The facts speak for themselves don't they? She's married to her Italian lover and my brother . . . or perhaps my half-brother is dead because of her . . .'

'Joel, you're not being logical,' Cassie interrupted sharply, knowing she was being cruel, but determined that he should be made to see the truth. 'Andrew died on his way to see your mother yes, but I've heard that he was always a reckless driver.' She had had that information from Mrs Pollit who, it seems, had never approved of him; and that he'd been drinking. 'Chances were that he would have had an accident of that sort anyway . . . the fact that he was on his way to Italy when it occurred was simply . . . unfortunate . . .' Before he could speak, she continued. 'The only reason your mother stayed with your father, Joel, was because of you . . . because she loved you very much . . . not because of what he owned, or her own status, or any other reason. Your father threatened to tell you that you weren't his son if she didn't stay. He blackmailed her, Joel, and for your sake she gave in . . .'

He went white and leaned over, gripping the side of her desk, his harsh, pain-filled 'No,' shuddering down her spine. The anguish in that denial would haunt her dreams for the rest of her life, Cassie thought achingly, wondering if she had done the right thing. Dark blue eyes burned into grey and she could almost feel Joel willing her to retract.

'If my father said that perhaps it was because he had good reason to suppose it was the truth . . .'

'Even if your mother had not told you that it wasn't, one look at the family portraits in the long gallery would be proof enough,' Cassie said quietly. 'Oh I know you have your mother's colouring, Joel, but physically you are very like some of your father's ancestors . . .'

His face still white, he stared at her and then without a word turned on his heel and left the room.

Cassie stayed where she was for several minutes before moving, worn out by the trauma of what had occurred. Did Joel believe her or would he simply go on denying the truth? It wouldn't be easy for him to accept, she acknowledged, and yet she sensed that until he did, until he came to terms with the fact that both his parents were humans, with human failings, he would continue to be tormented by the past.

It was only when she had said 'goodbye' to the last batch of guests that she realised Joel appeared to have gone. She had been so busy circulating and talking that she hadn't realised he wasn't about until now. A quick check of the downstairs room confirmed his absence. Could he have gone upstairs? Cassie frowned, hardly likely.

Putting on her coat she hurried round to the garages, her heart plummeting when she discovered that his car was gone, despair quickly giving way to anxious dread as she remembered how Andrew had died. Joel too had been drinking . . . and worse must be feeling emotionally disturbed. Anxiety gave way to guilt and Cassie paced the house, aching with restless energy long after the catering staff had gone.

Where was Joel? She rang his London flat, something she would never normally have done, too concerned over his safety to worry about what female might answer the 'phone, but the receiver remained lifeless. No one was there. What ought she to do? Ring the police? And say what? Darkness fell bringing with it a cooling breeze, but Cassie was unaware of the drop in temperature. Where was Joel? What had she done? She ought never to have spoken.

It was gone one before she finally sat down, subsiding on one of the settees in the salon and drawing herself up into a tiny ball, her eyes glued to the telephone, imagining with every heart-beat that it would ring and some impersonal voice on the other end would tell her that Joel had been involved in an accident.

At last she dozed off, exhausted by worry and fear, vivid images of Joel injured, perhaps even dead, tormenting her shallow rest. And it was all her fault. All of it.

CHAPTER TEN

'CASSIE.'

The low murmur of her name and the fingers resting on her shoulder brought her out of sleep. The room was in darkness, and her body felt stiff and cold. Even so hope flared warmly inside her, making her voice tremulous as she whispered, 'Joel? You're all right?' Tears flooded her eyes and she could hardly speak, her muffled, 'Oh thank God,' making the fingers on her shoulder tense slightly.

'You were worried?'

The curious inflection in his voice brought her back to reality, her body tensing as she tried to uncurl it and stand up. Her legs had gone semi-numb and as she tried to move she cried out in momentary pain as the blood started to flow back to her numbed limbs and they refused to support her when she tried to stand up.

'Cassie . . . Relax, it's all right . . .' Joel's arms came round her as he supported her weight, her head cradled against his shoulder. 'You ought to be in bed,' he told her and despite the darkness Cassie could sense him frowning. 'What were you doing sleeping down here . . .'

'It was an accident . . . I was . . . I was worried about you,' she admitted huskily. 'I . . .' she broke off to shiver involuntarily, remembering her torturing fears. Joel's arms tightened round her immediately. 'I'll take you upstairs,' he offered. 'You're frozen.'

Cassie knew that she should ask him to put her down, but the temptation to simply curl into his warmth and remain held in his arms was too much. She closed her eyes the better to savour the familiar scent of him, lost in a wave of yearning so intense that she didn't even realise they had reached her room until she felt the bed depress under her. Joel reached out to snap on the bedside lamp and Cassie recoiled from its brightness almost instinctively curling herself into a small, tight ball, her back to Joel and the lamp.

'You can't go to sleep like that,' Joel objected, and it seemed to Cassie in her sleepy state that there was an undercurrent of concerned tenderness to his protest. 'You'll freeze . . . Here let me help you . . .'

Firm hands rolled her over, but Cassie kept her eyes squeezed tightly closed. Fear and nervous exhaustion were both taking their toll; the day had been difficult enough without the added trauma of their quarrel—a trauma she had brought entirely on herself, she reminded herself self mockingly. But at least Joel was safe . . . As she remembered her fears, her body trembled, her fingers reaching out to grasp Joel's wrist, instinctively seeking the reassuring contact of his warm flesh.

'What's the matter? Light too bright?'

It was easier to agree than to explain the heart-swelling relief his presence brought her, reassuring her that he was alive and well and so Cassie simply nodded, keeping her eyes closed.

She felt the velvet blackness against their lids when Joel snapped off the lamp, and her skin prickled tormentingly as he murmured, 'There, that better?'

He was talking to her as though she were a cherished child, Cassie thought wonderingly, realising for the first time that something had changed, that his manner was different. She opened her eyes trying to sit up and discovering that Joel was sitting on the bed next to her.

'Joel . . .'

'Shush . . . don't talk now,' he told her. 'You're practically asleep. Let's get this off for you . . .'

His fingers moved deftly over buttons and fastenings and Cassie simply lay there, letting him take control, soothed by the cool comforting drift of his hands against her body, too emotionally drained to do more than give thanks that he was safe.

Her nightgown was a sliver of sea-foam-green silk, and she shivered as she felt the cool brush of it against her skin.

'This can't possibly keep you warm,' Joel's voice was husky, brushing arousingly over her raw nerves.

But Cassie managed to say valiantly, 'It isn't designed to.'

'Then there isn't much point in me putting it on you is there?' His voice was still husky, vibrating with a warmth that stirred a heat in the pit of Cassie's stomach. She kept her eyes closed as Joel pulled back the covers of her bed, and she slipped gratefully beneath them. Her sheets felt cold against her naked skin, tiredness pressing heavy weights down on her eyelids. She could hear vague sounds of movement, elusively familiar and yet somehow alien. There was a cold rush of night air as Joel lifted the covers a second time and she made a small murmur of protest.

'It's all right, Cassie.' His voice soothed and relaxed her and she made no protest when his arms came round her, drawing her back into the warmth of his body. In her half-awake state it did not seem at all strange that Joel should be in bed with her, warming her with the heat of his body, comforting her with the heavy thud of his heart under her cheek. As she drifted off to sleep she curled closer to him, murmuring soft sounds of pleasure, feeling the tension of the day slip away from her.

She was awake early, disturbed by the unfamiliar weight of Joel's arm beneath her breasts, his breath warm against the back of her neck. As she wriggled slightly away from him the events of the previous evening came storming back. She turned her head silently studying his sleeping, vulnerable features. A shadow darkened his jaw, and she reached out tentative fingers to touch the dark stubble, feeling it prickle against her skin. His eyelashes were long and thick, his hair ruffled. As though he missed her presence in his arms, he frowned and rolled towards her, his arm moving back from her waist to just below her breasts, his palm warm against the underside of one as his fingers cupped gently round it. He made small sounds of pleasure in his sleep, throwing one leg possessively across her body, pinning her to the bed. How she loved him, and how impossible that love was. Why had he stayed with her last night? Sighing, Cassie tried to view her future without him, and succeeded only in re-awakening the aching pain she had grown to live with recently. Her head nestled against his shoulder and if she turned her face towards him her lips were almost touching the strong, corded column of his throat. Almost instinctively Cassie found she was doing just that. His skin tasted warm, and faintly musky. Her tongue delicately explored the texture of it, her fingertips unconsciously stroking through the fine dark hair covering the exposed portion of his chest. The warmth of his body so close to hers made her ache in the pit of her stomach and she trembled drawing back from him, knowing that she could not trust herself not to betray her feelings if she stayed where she was. As she raised her head the dark lashes lifted, densely blue eyes trapping fleeing hazel ones.

'Don't stop,' Joel murmured softly, watching her intently.

'You were awake.' She said the words almost accusingly, colour storming her skin. Her tongue flicked nervously over her lips and caught the taste of him. Joel's concentration focused on her mouth, his hand lifting to thread through her hair. She knew that he would kiss her and that she ought to move but she couldn't. The touch of his mouth against hers, initially fleeting, almost testing, aroused a storm of need inside her, her lips clinging softly to his as her fingers curled tightly against his skin. His mouth moulded hers, gently at first, and then with growing passion as he found her lips warm and pliant beneath his, his teeth tugging, erotically inflicting tiny darts of pain that his tongue soothed as her lips parted for him.

His arms tightened possessively round her, his body pressing hers down into the bed, so that her own arms had no place to go other than round him, the harsh abrasion of his hair-coarsened flesh against her soft breasts accelerating the pace of her breathing until her body arched in mute invitation glorying in the downward sweep of his hands as they stroked and explored her feminine curves.

Joel groaned deeply in his throat as her hands slid over his back and down to his waist, the urgent movements of his body against hers making Cassie shiver in responsive pleasure.

'Touch me, Cassie,' he pleaded hoarsely against her mouth. 'I want to feel your hands on my body, your mouth against my skin.'

Mindlessly Cassie responded, allowing him to lead her deeper and deeper along paths of sensual discovery, expressing her love for him with every caress of her hands and lips, the hoarse groans of pleasure lost against her body with every heated thrust of Joel's making her almost feverish in her desire to please him. He was so strong, and yet so vulnerable, trembling almost beneath the lightest touch of her hands. The harsh clamour of the front door bell intruding on their privacy shocked Cassie into tense stillness, her eyes shamed and wary as she avoided Joel's. What must he think of her? Instinctively she moved away from him, covering her nudity, hearing him swear briefly as he got out of bed.

Cassie had no idea who could be calling so early in the day and she lay, frozen beneath the bedclothes as Joel pulled on the clothes he had discarded the night before.

'Cassie . . .' he paused by the door, but she couldn't bring herself to look at him, and then the bell pealed again.

'You'd better go and answer it.' How cool and composed she sounded, in direct contrast to how she felt.

She heard Joel open the door and then the sound of voices, indistinguishable to her other than a low hum of noise. Curiosity drove her from her bed and into her bathroom, where she showered, quickly dressing in pretty cotton jeans and a matching shirt.

The study door was open when she got downstairs and she walked in, coming to an abrupt halt as she took in the scene there. Miranda was standing within the circle of Joel's arms, smiling up at him while Nico looked on indulgently.

Completely bewildered Cassie stared from Miranda to Joel. Smiling tearfully Miranda broke away from her son and stretched out her arms to Cassie. 'Oh Cassie, my dear, what can I say?' she asked softly.

What were Miranda and Nico doing here? Cassie looked at Joel, but his expression was unreadable.

'When Joel rang me last night I could hardly believe it,' Miranda told Cassie softly. 'Oh Cassie, I can't tell you how happy I am. Nico and I decided to fly over straight away. I had to see Joel for myself.'

'I . . .' Joel had rung Miranda last night?

'I haven't had a chance yet to tell Cassie that I spoke to you,' Joel interrupted. 'I was so furious with you for what you said to me that I had to get away,' he told Cassie quietly. 'I got in the car and simply drove around—for almost two hours, thinking, going over what you'd said, until I realised I simply had to know the truth ... I stopped at a small hotel and rang Florence.'

'I couldn't believe it when the 'phone rang and it was Joel,' Miranda interrupted excitedly. 'He told me what you'd said to him, Cassie, and asked me if it was true. Long ago I recognised the harm I'd done by trying to protect his father, and so I told him the whole story.'

'And I found myself listening and believing,' Joel cut in. 'Perhaps I'd known in my heart of hearts all along that my father's version of events was biased, but ...'

'But you couldn't forgive me for what you saw as my betrayal,' Miranda said softly. 'You thought I hadn't cared about you.'

'I was jealous,' Joel admitted. 'Jealous of the fact that another man meant more to you than your husband and children; than me, and that jealousy had stayed with me as an adult, tainting my whole attitude towards women. I admit that now ...'

'I simply couldn't wait to see him,' Miranda told Cassie. 'I had to see him for myself, to believe that it was true ... that he'd forgiven me at long last.'

'There was nothing to forgive,' Joel said quietly.

A deep sense of loneliness swept over Cassie. She felt excluded from the happy family circle, an outsider, whose part in their drama was over, and who was now superfluous to events. Joel didn't need her any more; after last night his company would be assured of all the financing it needed; enough faith had been expressed in his current project for her to be sure of that. Her angry revelation of the truth had helped to heal the breach between him and Miranda—Joel no longer needed her as his wife. She emerged from her deeply morose thoughts to hear Nico saying genially, 'No, I insist lunch must be my treat, but I must rely on you, Joel, to suggest an appropriate venue.'

'There's a very good hotel not far from here— an old country house in a very attractive gardens. I'll give them a ring . . .'

He picked up the 'phone and Cassie heard him book a table for four. So she was to be included in the luncheon party. She shrank from going; from witnessing their happiness when she felt so miserable. She knew now why Joel had been so kind to her last night, and again this morning. He was grateful to her. She could see it in the way he looked at her and it touched her heart with bitterness.

She waited until he had hung up to say casually, 'I'd rather not go if you don't mind, Joel . . . I'm rather behind on my work, it will give me a chance to catch up.' She turned away from him as she spoke and missed his quick frown.

'But, *cara* . . .' Miranda pleaded, only to fall silent as Cassie flashed her a determinedly bright smile, and said quickly,

'No, please . . . this is essentially a family celebration. I should only feel awkward, and I really must do some work.' Her mouth went dry with tension in the heavy silence that followed.

'But, Cassie . . .' Joel started to object until Miranda cut in quietly,

'Don't push her, Joel, if Cassie doesn't want to join us, she must be allowed not to do so. In fact it might be as well if we left her now to get on with her work.' She slipped her arm through Joel's as she spoke, and Cassie knew if they stayed any longer she would betray herself by breaking down in tears. She couldn't bear the hurt in Miranda's eyes, nor the anger in Joel's, but neither could she endure sitting across a table from Joel trying to appear light-hearted and happy all the time knowing that her time with him was quickly coming to an end.

It was only when the others had departed for their lunch that Cassie realised what she ought to do. It would be the wisest and most sensible course, and yet she shrank from it, putting it off until she knew she could delay no longer. Upstairs in her room she found her suitcase, and slowly started packing. Totally engrossed in her task and her own misery she didn't realise she was no longer alone until her bedroom door was abruptly thrust open. She looked up from her kneeling position on the floor beside her case to find Joel glaring down at her.

'And just what do you think you're doing?' he gritted furiously.

Trying to hold on to her self-control Cassie said as lightly as she could. 'I should have thought it was obvious, I'm packing my clothes . . .'

'Sneaking away behind my back you mean?'

'Why aren't you with your mother,' Cassie retorted wildly, not wishing to continue such a potentially dangerous conversation.

'Because I learned from her something so important, that I had to come back and test its veracity for myself,' Joel told her softly. 'Cassie, why are you packing?'

'You don't need me any more,' she told him without daring to look at him. 'You have sufficient financial backing for your projects now . . .'

'And if I did need you?' He asked the question softly, dropping down beside her on the floor, and pushing aside her case, his fingers cupping her jaw so that she was forced to look at him.

'What could you possibly need me for now?' she scoffed, trying not to tremble. 'You have everything you want . . .'

'Not everything.'

The heat of his fingers caressing her skin was making her shake, her body aching with hunger for him. Another moment and she would betray herself completely. She tried to pull away, tensing as he demanded thickly, 'Why did you let me make love to you . . .'

What could she say? She shrugged, and tried to appear nonchalant. 'Everyone has to start somewhere?'

'And that's all it was? Curiosity . . . a desire to experiment?' That couldn't possibly be pain harshening his voice.

Cassie shrugged again. 'Why not? After all you made love to me too and you can hardly claim that it was because you found me irresistible.'

'Can't I?'

The husky question shocked her into stunned silence, pain flaring to life deep in her eyes.

'Stop it,' she demanded wildly. 'Stop doing

this to me. You didn't even spare me a second look until you came to Florence, and found me with Bernardo. You married me because you wanted my company; my computer skill . . .'

Hard fingers bit into her shoulders as Joel stood up, dragging her up with him. 'I planned to marry you for that reason yes,' he grated harshly. 'I'd assessed you as a cold, emotionless female ready to exchange her skills in return for a husband, but the reality totally threw me. You were so prickly and defensive; you valued yourself so little. It infuriated me that you should have so low an opinion of yourself; that I should want you, when I had proved immune to so many other women.'

His thumb was probing the soft fullness of her lips and Cassie stared up at him disbelievingly.

'You didn't even see me as a woman until I came back from Florence,' she accused trying to escape the sensual spell he was weaving around her.

'Wrong,' Joel told her softly. 'I saw you very much as a woman right from the start. A woman who hid her femininity away from the world, it's true, but a very feminine, vulnerable woman despite that, and one who had a dangerous hold on my senses. It infuriated me that I should want you; that my emotions were clouding my judgment to the extent where I was prepared to risk all my careful plans for the future simply because of my need to hold you in my arms.'

'You're just saying that because you feel sorry for me,' Cassie interrupted flatly, 'because Miranda told you that . . .'

'That what?' he prompted softly. 'That you love me? Is that it, Cassie?'

The soft mockery in his voice drove her beyond the edge of caution. 'Yes ... yes, damn you,' she stormed bitterly at him. 'Yes I love you ... but you needn't think ...'

She gasped as the hard pressure of his mouth stemmed her words, his groaned, 'Cassie ... Cassie, how can you be so intelligent and such a fool,' he muttered against her lips, and then he was kissing her as she had dreamed of him doing; with passion and hunger, and a need that drove her weak body into yielding acceptance of the hard pressure of his as she clung to him, returning the feverish intensity of his kiss, drowning herself in the surging pleasure of it, telling herself that nothing else mattered.

'Cassie, Cassie, how could you not know that I love you?' Joel muttered shakily as he released her. 'Why on earth did you think I made love to you?'

'I thought you didn't realise it was me ... you said nothing ...'

'Because I thought I'd alienated you ... hurt you ... driven you away from me with the selfishness of my need to possess you. I felt guilty, can't you understand that?' He sighed, resting his forehead against hers, as he said in a low voice. 'Do you honestly think that if anyone other than you had said what you did about my parents that I'd have believed them? It was only because it was you, Cassie, that I thought deeply about it; that I decided to speak to my mother. If it had been anyone else I wouldn't have listened. I think I was half way to falling in love with you when I decided to marry you. The company was just a convenient excuse, but every time I touched you or came near you you rejected me . . .'

'Because I was frightened of betraying my feelings . . . I thought you despised me . . . I was so plain and dull.'

'No. You must never think that. You didn't know how to use your natural advantages. Perhaps now you do, but you were never plain; never dull.' He kissed her lightly and then more lingeringly before saying musingly, 'I seem to remember that you and I have some unfinished business.'

When Cassie glanced uncomprehendingly at him, he laughed softly. 'We were interrupted at a most inopportune time this morning, wouldn't you agree?'

He laughed again when Cassie blushed. 'Your mother,' she protested weakly, 'they'll be back soon. Oh, and Joel, what must she think of me, refusing to have lunch with you, and then you leaving them to come back here.'

'She was the one who told me to come back, when she realised how restless and morose I was.'

'And she told you that I loved you?'

'She suggested that we might both be suffering from the same malady,' he agreed, 'and since I already knew what mine was, it didn't take long for me to deduce the identity of yours. Do you love me, Cassie?'

'Didn't I tell you how much, without words, this morning,' she whispered shyly, bending her head so that he could barely catch the words. His smile set her heart pounding with delirious anticipation.

'I think you'd better refresh my memory,' he suggested with mock gravity, picking her up in his arms and heading for the bed, 'starting right at the beginning.'

'If that's what you really want,' Cassie began docilely, only to blush vividly as he bent his head and whispered against her ear exactly what it was he wanted of her,

'And that's just for starters,' he added softly, watching her bright colour subside.

You're invited to accept 4 books and a surprise gift Free!

Acceptance Card

Mail to: **Harlequin Reader Service®**

In the U.S.
2504 West Southern Ave.
Tempe, AZ 85282

In Canada
P.O. Box 2800, Postal Station A
5170 Yonge Street
Willowdale, Ontario M2N 6J3

YES! Please send me 4 free Harlequin Presents® novels and my free surprise gift. Then send me 8 brand new novels every month as they come off the presses. Bill me at the low price of $1.75 each ($1.95 in Canada)—an 11% saving off the retail price. There are no shipping, handling or other hidden costs. There is no minimum number of books I must purchase. I can always return a shipment and cancel at any time. Even if I never buy another book from Harlequin, the 4 free novels and the surprise gift are mine to keep forever.

108 BPP-BPGE

Name	(PLEASE PRINT)

Address	Apt. No.

City	State/Prov.	Zip/Postal Code

This offer is limited to one order per household and not valid to present subscribers. Price is subject to change.
ACP-SUB-1

EYE OF THE STORM

MAURA SEGER

A powerful
portrayal of
the events of
World War II in the
Pacific, *Eye of the Storm* is a riveting story of how love
triumphs over hatred. In this, the first of a three-book
chronicle, Army nurse Maggie Lawrence meets Marine
Sgt. Anthony Gargano. Despite military regulations
against fraternization, they resolve to face together
whatever lies ahead.... Author Maura Seger, also known
to her fans as Laurel Winslow, Sara Jennings, Anne
MacNeil and Jenny Bates, was named 1984's
Most Versatile Romance Author by *The Romantic Times*.

*You're invited to accept
4 books and a
surprise gift* **Free!**

Acceptance Card

Mail to: Harlequin Reader Service®

In the U.S.
2504 West Southern Ave.
Tempe, AZ 85282

In Canada
P.O. Box 2800, Postal Station A
5170 Yonge Street
Willowdale, Ontario M2N 6J3

YES! Please send me 4 free Harlequin Romance® novels and my free surprise gift. Then send me 6 brand new novels every month as they come off the presses. Bill me at the low price of $1.65 each ($1.75 in Canada) — an 11% saving off the retail price. There are no shipping, handling or other hidden costs. There is no minimum number of books I must purchase. I can always return a shipment and cancel at any time. Even if I never buy another book from Harlequin, the 4 free novels and the surprise gift are mine to keep forever.

116 BPR-BPGE

Name	(PLEASE PRINT)	
Address		Apt. No.
City	State/Prov.	Zip/Postal Code

This offer is limited to one order per household and not valid to present subscribers. Price is subject to change.

ACR-SUB-1